Sophie's Adventures in Time

BEVERLY PARKHURST MOSS

Archway Publishing books may be ordered through booksellers or by contacting:

Archway Publishing
1663 Liberty Drive
Bloomington, IN 47403
www.archwaypublishing.com
844-669-3957

Because of the dynamic nature of the Internet, any web addresses or links contained in this book may have changed since publication and may no longer be valid. The views expressed in this work are solely those of the author and do not necessarily reflect the views of the publisher, and the publisher hereby disclaims any responsibility for them.

Any people depicted in stock imagery provided by Getty Images are models, and such images are being used for illustrative purposes only. Certain stock imagery © Getty Images.

ISBN: 978-1-6657-1966-7 (sc)
ISBN: 978-1-6657-1965-0 (hc)
ISBN: 978-1-6657-1967-4 (e)

Library of Congress Control Number: 2022903603

Print information available on the last page.

Archway Publishing rev. date: 04/11/2022

Part One

Introduction

Sophie's Adventure in Time is a fictional story that contains actual Texas history along with a variety of Texas heroes and villains.

The idea for this story all started years ago when my friend Brenda Briscoe and I were driving from Austin to Dallas. She suggested we stop at the small town of Salado to have lunch at the Stagecoach Inn. When we arrived at the hotel, the first thing I noticed was an amazing tree in the courtyard. Some of the branches were so large they were supported by iron stakes. When I asked our waitress about the tree, she told us she thought it was approximately six hundred years old. I've always been fascinated by small towns, and I love history. I was an incorrigible tree climber as a child, so, needless to say, I like trees.

Texas has a fascinating history that includes an abundance of eccentric and colorful characters. Many of them were good and others bad. The one thing they all had in common was they were not boring.

Over the years, I thought about that tree, that wonderful hotel, and the colorful town of Salado located in the southern part of Texas.

I've always been the storyteller in my family, and I decided I wanted to write a book for my grandchildren – the youngest ones are now in their teens. Hopefully, it would be a book they would pass on to their children.

As the characters of Sophie, her parents, her pets, her Sudanese friend Amy, and Presley, along with others, began to take on life in my imagination, I needed to find the right setting. The story begins in Dallas, Texas, but much of it takes place in Salado, Texas.

The references to Sophie's mother's publishing company are strictly fictional.

One of the children is Amy who is the daughter of a Sudanese refugee. Amy is real. I met her when she was a little girl while writing the book *Dark Exodus, the Lost Girls of Sudan*.

After finishing *Sophie's Adventure in Time*, I can honestly say, even though I didn't move to Texas until 1961, I would not want to live anywhere else.

Chapter 1

My name is Sophie, and I'm twelve years old. I am just a kid, and I should be talking to my friends about slumber parties, going to Six Flags (the best amusement park in the world), or sitting in the large swing on our porch in the old house I used to live in. But the house is gone, my friends are gone, and worst of all, my mom is gone. She didn't have a disease or an accident. She simply disappeared. The only good thing is my dad is back. He was missing for months, and everyone but me thought he was dead. He says we are survivors. Even though I always agree with him, I'm not sure if I'm a survivor, but I won't tell him that. He's been through enough, and I'm all he has left.

My dad and I are headed to the Texas Hill Country town of Salado in our old Jeep. The heat is shimmering and bouncing off the hot asphalt as we speed along the interstate. Horses, long-horned cattle, ranches, farms, weathered barns, and falling-down sheds long abandoned appear then disappear, as if by magic. Slumped down in my seat, much of this barely registers because my brain is like a merry-go-round as it spins in circles going nowhere. One scene after another flashes through my mind. I see my mother brushing her long red hair and laughing. Then there's the parade of cops going in and out of that lovely old house in the Lakewood area of Dallas, Texas, that we lived in right after she vanished. They questioned me over and over. I couldn't tell them anything because to this day, I don't know anything. Another Technicolor slide jumps into my brain. It's a scene of Aunt Rose banishing me to my room without dinner. For a long time, I hated her. That picture fades to be replaced by Uncle Bob. His blue eyes sparkle behind his glasses as he smiles at me. He and Mabel, the cook, were my silent supporters in a house that was like one of those fake cakes you see in bakery windows. Frosted on the outside, it looks delicious, but when you cut into it, there is nothing underneath but cardboard. Determined to shake off those depressing thoughts, I force myself to return to the present.

Dad used to laugh a lot, but he doesn't laugh much anymore. I notice how pale he is as he grips the steering wheel and stares straight ahead. He walks with a limp, and there are worry lines between his eyebrows. He's thinner, and there are a few gray hairs in his sideburns. He survived Afghanistan after being wounded only to come home and find his world destroyed. He went through a lot in the military. I have asked him questions, but it is obvious he doesn't want to talk about that part of his life. If I didn't know better, I would think he's angry. When we're together, there are long stretches of silence. Sometimes he just sits and stares into space. Often, his eyes are sad when he looks at me. Worst of all are the nights when he yells in his sleep. He has terrible nightmares, and when I wake him up, for those first few minutes, he stares at me as if he doesn't know who I am.

When I was little, I never got mad. Now I get angry a lot. I even beat up a girl in school. Even though she had it coming, I shouldn't have done it. As these memories flash through my mind, I realize I'm fighting tears, but I am determined that I am not going to cry. It would upset my dad. I don't want to make him sadder than he already is.

When we get to Salado, we'll check into the Stagecoach Inn. Dad and his friend Mike have started a new virtual magazine and a website called Texas Trails. Salado is the first Texas town we're featuring, and the Stagecoach Inn is the cover story. I'm glad that Bingo and Bo Jangles are with me. Dad says we won't stay anywhere pets aren't allowed. "After what you've been through, Sophie, you need your pets," he said when we started out. Even though he is sad, and half the time I can't figure out if I am sad or mad, I'm excited about this trip because he is excited.

"This is a new beginning," he announced earlier. "Even though we lost everything, we're starting over. Mike is a great friend. I couldn't do this without him."

I agree. Mike was Mom's editor for the magazine she published before everything fell apart. The format of Texas Trails features Texas towns, out of the way places, and points of interest. We are getting lots of hits on the internet, and we're building a large audience. Dad says it appeals to people who like Texas history and want to travel.

I glance over at him again. His profile shows a strong jaw, high cheekbones, and dark hair. Mom used to say my dad was tall, dark, and drop-dead handsome. His name is Christian, but everyone calls him Chris.

Mom's name is Rachael, but her friends call her Ray. She's a natural red head, and she's beautiful. People say she has charisma. I don't know what that means exactly, but I think it's because she is outgoing and sees the best in people.

When it comes to looks, I don't know what happened to me. Almost white, my hair is thick and curly, and it stands up all over my head. Mom used to laugh and say it was my halo. "That's proof you're an angel," she said more than once. I'm skinny, and my knees are knobby. Mom says I have beautiful eyes – they're green, but I wear glasses. Hopefully, next year I'll get contacts.

Leaning back in my seat, I close my eyes and pretend to be asleep as I think about everything that's happened. I've decided that someday I'll be a writer, and one of the first things I'll do is write my life's story. It's important not to forget anything. Mom used to say writers need a good story line. Mine is one I'd rather be without. The plot is clouded with mysteries. The biggest mystery is the disappearance of my mother. I am determined to find answers. This means I must go back to the beginning.

Chapter 2

My story began in an old, two-story house with a big porch located in Lakewood, one of the oldest neighborhoods in Dallas. Growing up in that house, I have a lot of happy memories. Our yard was huge. I was six when Dad built the treehouse. It had steps that started at the base of the tree and wound all the way around the trunk to the top. During the summer, the branches shaded our whole back yard. I lugged dolls, dishes, and even small furniture into my treehouse, where I would host tea parties. It was one of my favorite places.

Like most kids, my biggest concerns were about my pets, my friends, and school. For as long as I can remember, Mom tucked me into bed at night and listened to my prayers. I never could keep secrets from her and always ended up confessing if I had done something wrong. Instead of scolding me, she would ask questions. Those questions led me to realize why my actions hurt not only me but sometimes others. "I can't always control your actions, Sophie," she would say, "but think about what you do because you can't always control the consequences of those actions."

"Why am I so ugly and skinny?" I often complained. "You're beautiful, and Dad is handsome. Everyone says so. I don't look anything like either one of you."

"Sophie, you look just like your father's mother. She was a beauty and had hair just like yours. You may be thin now, but some day you will have a beautiful figure. Right now, you're like a colt standing on wobbly legs, but mark my words, when you grow up, you'll be a beautiful racehorse. The most important thing is that you have God in your heart. That gives you your own special beauty."

Somehow, Mom always made me feel better. A lot of kids complain about their mothers. I never did because my mom was my best friend. She was the coolest mom any kid could ever have.

I also have the coolest pets. Bo Jangles is the smartest cat in the world, and Bingo is the silliest dog. When Bingo was a puppy, Mom found him in a box in an alley behind a restaurant. We ran ads and posted fliers. When there was no response, we decided to keep him. At first, we thought he was a Chihuahua. As he got older, he grew whiskers and a mustache. In many ways, he's a living cartoon. His personality is huge.

Bo Jangles was another rescue. We woke up one morning and found a tiny kitten sitting on our front porch. He looked like he was only five or six weeks old. It's turned out he is a hybrid Bengal. He has a low voice and deep growl. He totally controls Bingo. Every morning when they're done eating, Bingo will run over to kiss Bo Jangles. Bo kisses him back, then hisses and slaps him on the nose. Bingo runs over to anyone who happens to be handy, whimpering and crying. The routine never changes. "I don't know if that dog is confused, stupid, or just very persistent," my dad says. Mom hung a bell on the door, and when Bo Jangles wanted to go outside, he jumped up and hit it until someone opened the door. Not only does Bo Jangles walk on a leash, he also fetches. Sometimes, when I was outside in the back yard, I would look up and see him peering down at me from the roof. I would raise my arms, and after a little coaxing, he would jump and land on my shoulder. Even though Bo Jangles smacks Bingo in the face, I know he loves him because he grooms him every day. I think he just wants to make sure Bingo knows he's in charge.

For years, my life went on uneventfully as spring blended into summer, summer into fall, and then into winter with the occasional ice storm. In July and August in Texas, there are days when you can fry an egg on the sidewalk. In winter, snow is a mainstream news headline. There is a saying in Texas, "If you don't like the weather, just hang around."

Chapter 3

I remember how excited Mom and I used to get when we found out Dad was coming home on leave. The last time I was that excited I was in the back yard when I heard Mom's cell phone ringing in the kitchen. "Tomorrow?" I heard her say. She sounded so excited that it could only mean one thing. After she put the phone down, she ran outside. There was a huge grin on her face. She grabbed my hands and swung me around in a circle. "Your daddy is coming home," she yelled.

Not only was I happy, I was relieved. Mom hadn't been herself for weeks. I knew something was wrong. She seemed distracted, and there were dark shadows under her eyes. Each day, she seemed more and more distant. One day I told her I had made a new friend. "That's nice, dear," she replied. Usually, she wanted to know every detail. I could tell my announcement didn't even register with her. In fact, I don't think she even heard me. It was as if her mind was a million miles away.

That same evening, I overheard Mom talking on the phone. I could tell she was upset. To my amazement, before slamming down the phone, she yelled, using words I had never heard her say. Later that night, I woke up to see a sliver of light seeping under my bedroom door. Curious, I got up and went to the kitchen. Sitting at the bar, Mom was nursing a cup of hot tea. I could tell she had been crying. Baffled, I just stood there for a few minutes. "Is Dad OK?" I asked.

"Don't worry, darling. Dad is fine." Finally, I went back to bed. Before drifting off to sleep, I said a prayer. "Please, God, let Dad get home soon. I know when he finds out what's upsetting Mom, he'll fix it."

My new friend's name was Sheila. She and her mother, brother, and stepfather had just moved into an apartment building a few streets over. I met her one day when I was walking Bingo. I had leaned down to pick up a pretty stone when Bingo gave a jerk, causing his leash to slip out of my hand. He ran right into the middle of the street. With a dopey grin on his face, he sat down wagging his tail furiously. I called him several times, but he just sat there. I think he thought we were playing a game. When I went to get him, I slipped and fell, skinning my knees. I was so mad I almost started to cry. Suddenly, a tall girl came sprinting through traffic. She grabbed Bingo's leash. "Come on you stupid, damn dog," she yelled. "Are you OK?" she asked when she reached me and leaned over to help me brush the dirt and gravel off my knees.

"I think my dog's retarded. Thank you for catching him." Even though Sheila was older than I was, this was the beginning of our friendship.

Sheila's hair was different lengths, and it was dyed pink. She wore black lipstick and black fingernail polish. She always wore black T-shirts and baggy pants. I had never known anyone like her. I thought she was interesting. For one thing, she used a lot of swear words. She also smoked. One day, she offered me a cigarette. Not wanting to appear dumb, I took it. After she lit it, I inhaled, taking a deep breath. A minute later, I was lying on the ground choking with tears running down my face. "You're such a baby," Sheila said after she quit laughing. She told me her mom and stepdad fought all the time, and her stepdad drank too much beer. When I asked her if she had met any of the older kids in the neighborhood, she replied, "Yes, and they're all losers and idiots." When I wanted to know more, she got mad and left.

"Where are you going?" I yelled at her retreating back. "I didn't mean to make you mad."

"I'll see you tomorrow if you quit asking so many damn questions."

"Sorry," I said in a small voice, at the same time wondering what I had done to upset her.

I didn't talk about Sheila to Mom because not only did it seem like her mind was always somewhere else, deep in my heart I knew she would not approve. For the first time in my life, I was keeping a secret. Normally, this would have bothered me. Instead, I felt a smug feeling of satisfaction. Mom and I used to go shopping, go to lunch at our favorite restaurants, and visit friends. I loved going to her office. It was exciting, especially at deadline times. The phones rang constantly, and there was always something new going on.

After getting the call from Dad, Mom seemed like her old self. Bingo and Bo Jangles seemed to know Dad was coming home, too. Bingo ran around in circles, and Bo Jangles jumped three feet in the air. The next day, we got up early, determined to beat the traffic on our way to the airport. "Can't you drive a little faster, Mom?" I asked as we turned onto the highway to the airport.

"And get stopped for speeding?" She did speed up, though, because she was as anxious to see Dad as I was. As we pulled up to the curb at Dallas-Fort Worth Airport, we saw him rushing out the revolving doors. Heads turned as people looked at my dad. He was wearing his uniform, and his good looks drew a lot of attention. He seemed oblivious to the stares. I thought my heart would burst with pride. I had no way of knowing this visit would be the last time the three of us would be together.

You've heard that saying, time flies? It certainly flew when Dad was home. Some nights we would stay home while Mom cooked Dad's favorite dishes. Mom called these evenings our date nights. We would dress up, and I would set the table using the best china, silver, and candles. Dad also would dress up. He held both of our chairs for us when we sat down, and he referred to us as his two beauties. Somehow, he always managed to make me feel pretty, even though I know I'm not.

Once word got out that Dad was home, there was always a steady stream of visitors. Mike, who was Mom's editor, always came, and the last time Dad came home, so did her new partner, Bill Crankshaw. But this time, Bill did not show up. Mom didn't say anything, but I think she was relieved. I thought back to the incident that happened during his last visit. Bingo, who usually seemed delighted to see visitors and often plopped down at their feet and rolled over for a belly rub, had taken one look at Mom's partner and started to growl. Before we could stop him, he lunged and grabbed his pant leg. I screamed when I realized he was going to kick Bingo. Bill stopped himself just in time. Grabbing Bingo, I hurried down the hall.

"Bill, I am so sorry," I heard Mom say as I left the room. "I don't know what's gotten into that dog."

"I guess the mutt is a good watchdog even though he is the ugliest dog I've ever seen," he replied.

"Don't worry, Bingo. You have a warrior's heart," I had whispered in his ear as he licked my face, and his brown eyes looked anxiously into mine. Now, thinking about Crankshaw's absence, I wondered if he didn't come because he didn't like dogs.

The night before Dad was supposed to get back to his base, I saw him sitting on the porch swing holding Mom's hand. Her face was white, and it was obvious he was furious. "Ray, you're too trusting," I heard him say. "You only see the good in people. Don't do anything just yet. I'm going to call in some favors. I'll deal with that jerk when I get back."

After Dad left, Mom slipped back into what almost seemed like a coma. She would sit for hours drinking coffee and staring into space. For the first time I could remember, she was staying home. She even started spending a lot of time in bed, something I had never seen her do. I was worried, but at times, I resented her.

I began spending more time with Sheila. "I don't know what's wrong with Mom," I confided. "She's acting even more strangely now that Dad has gone back to Afghanistan."

"Your mom and dad must have had a fight. They're probably going to get a divorce."

For a minute, I was too shocked to reply. "That will never happen." I said, my voice high. "They never fight."

"My folks fight all the time. Believe me, all married people fight. My mom's been divorced four times."

I didn't respond, but I knew Sheila was wrong. My parents loved each other.

One day, Sheila and I wandered into the drugstore. I loved looking at the various colors of lipstick and nail polish. When I turned to point out the black nail polish that was Sheila's favorite, to my surprise, she had walked away. A few minutes later, she reappeared. "Do you have any Kleenex?" she asked. Still looking at the array of colors, I mindlessly handed her my purse. Suddenly, she said, "We need to leave."

"Let's stay a minute. Look at these latest arrivals. Aren't they neat?"

Without a word, she grabbed my hand and almost jerked me out the front door. We had only taken a few steps when one of the clerks from the drugstore ran up behind us. "Stop!" he yelled. I turned around and looked at him in amazement.

Sheila acted like she didn't hear him and kept walking. I stood there in shock as he grabbed her by the arm and jerked her back until she was standing beside me. "Shoplifting is a crime," he said, looking at us in disgust.

"I would never shoplift," I stammered.

"Oh, no? Let's take a look." Grabbing my purse, he opened it. There sat three bottles of nail polish and two lipsticks. I was so stunned, I couldn't respond.

"You're coming back to the store," the clerk announced. "The manager has called the police." My heart sank. Meanwhile, Sheila refused to look at me. Bewildered, I tried to hold back the tears as we were marched back into the drugstore. Sitting in the manager's office, I felt totally humiliated. I could only stare at the floor. This was the drugstore where my mother shopped. Now, I would be branded as a thief. "How could Sheila do this to me?" I wondered. "I thought she was my friend."

When the manager left the room for a moment I glared at Sheila. "REALLY, SHEILA? SOME FRIEND YOU TURNED OUT TO BE."

"Just be cool; you'll be OK. Your family's rich, and your mom is popular. You've always had everything. You're nothing but a punk kid. Actually, you're a spoiled brat."

Stunned, I was speechless. I couldn't help but wonder if she had ever even liked me at all. Now I understood why she hung around with me even though I was younger. The kids her age probably wouldn't have anything to do with her.

The policeman was stern. When we got to the police station, we were put in separate rooms. After what seemed like forever, a policewoman came in and sat down across from me. "Your friend says she put the cosmetics in your purse without you knowing it. We've had problems with Sheila before. I suggest you stay away from her because she's nothing but trouble. I've called your mother to pick you up. She's done a lot for the community, so you're free to go. If your friend had not admitted that she put those things in your purse, you could have ended up in juvenile detention. Believe me, that would not have been a pleasant experience."

I was relieved when Mom walked through the door, but when I took one look at her face, I knew she was furious. In the car, I started to explain as she stared silently ahead. "Go to your room," she said once we got home. "You're grounded for two weeks. I'm very disappointed in you. As for that girl – you won't be seeing her again."

For some reason, even though she had betrayed me, I felt the need to defend Sheila. "She's not a bad person," I yelled.

"Is that so? Then why haven't you brought her home and introduced her to me? You knew I wouldn't approve of her. As for being a friend – what kind of person gets a friend in trouble by shoplifting and putting stuff in her friend's purse. You will not be seeing her again, and that's that."

"I told you about her, and you didn't even listen. You never listen to me anymore." Suddenly, all the fear, frustration, and anger boiled over. As I rushed down the hall to my room, I yelled, "I hate you," before throwing myself on the bed. Tears ran down my face as I thought about the events that had transpired during what had started out as a typical summer day. I thought Sheila liked me. Why had she shoplifted, and why would she want to get me in trouble?

Later, Mom came into my room carrying a glass of milk and a sandwich. Sitting down on the bed, she stroked my hair. "Sophie, you are a good person, and I know this was not your fault. One of the most painful things in life is betrayal, especially when it's by someone you think is a friend. Sad to say, I'm still learning that lesson. I'm not judging Sheila. In fact, I feel sorry for her. From what I understand she has a rough home life. It seems everyone in her family has been in trouble with the law at one time or another. Even though she got you in trouble, she did the right thing by admitting she put those things in your purse without you knowing it. I'm sorry I've neglected you. Someday I'll tell you why. I promise I'll try to do better."

Not saying a word, I lay with my face turned to the wall. After a few minutes, Mom got up and left the room. As I thought about what she said, I realized she was right. I remembered what she had said about consequences. Now I knew that having a friend who gets you in trouble can have its own set of consequences. I wondered what Mom meant when she said she was still learning about betrayal by a friend. "I'll apologize in the morning," I told myself before I drifted to sleep.

Chapter 4

In the middle of the night, I woke up to hear Bingo growling. He was barking as he ran around in circles in front of the closed bedroom door. Bo Jangles, standing motionless on the pillow next to me, was staring fixedly at the door. With his tail puffed out and his ears flattened, he was letting out a deep, throaty growl. Sitting up, I rubbed my eyes. "What is going on?" I wondered sleepily. I remembered hearing noises a few nights earlier. When I had looked out the window, I had seen an owl sitting on a branch. The wind was causing another branch to hit the window, which made a scratchy sound.

"It's probably that stupid owl again," I told myself. "Be quiet, Bingo," I ordered sternly. He finally quit barking but continued to whine. Bo Jangles went under the bed and refused to come out. "Darned old owl," I told myself sleepily before I fell asleep again. "I hope it finds another tree. I'm going to tell Mom that branch needs to be cut."

When I woke up the next morning, the sun was streaming through the window. I had overslept. Ever since I could remember, I had awakened to the delicious aroma of coffee floating down the hall. Now, not only did I not smell the coffee, I didn't hear Mom moving around the kitchen as she prepared breakfast. The house seemed eerily still – almost as if it was holding its breath waiting for something to happen.

"Mom?" I called. Silence. Getting up, I put on my slippers and went to her bedroom. I could smell the trace of her perfume on the sheets of her unmade bed. There was the usual pile of books on the nightstand

and an open Ken Follett novel lying on the covers. Her purse was on the antique dresser.

Mystified, I wandered through the house. It was empty. I went to the garage. Mom's red SUV was parked in its usual place. I wandered back to the kitchen. I wished I was still asleep and that this was all a dream. Closing my eyes, I willed Mom to return. In my mind, I could imagine her laughing as she rushed into the room. She would make French toast, or maybe we would go out to breakfast.

After what seemed like an eternity, I opened my eyes. Surrounded by the terrible silence, the minutes slowly ticked by on the kitchen clock as my confusion turned to dread. I remembered Bingo growling and barking during the night and Bo Jangles hiding under the bed. Something bad had happened. I just didn't know what.

Minutes later, I ran across the yard and banged on the neighbor's door. Mr. and Mrs. Jones were not only our neighbors, they were friends.

"What is it, Sophie?" Mr. Jones asked as he opened the door. When he saw the look on my face, his expression turned to one of concern.

"Have you seen Mom? Her purse is on her dresser, and her car is in the garage, but I can't find her anywhere. I know she wouldn't go off without telling me where she was going. Something has happened to her."

"I'm sure there's a good explanation," Mr. Jones said. "Why don't you come in. Have you eaten?"

By this time, I could barely hold back the tears. Mrs. Jones tried to console me as she placed a glass of milk, a plate of toast, and a jar of jam on the table in front of me. The worried look on her face and the quaver in her voice told me she was worried, too. Meanwhile, I could hear Mr. Jones speaking softly but insistently on the phone. I knew he didn't want to worry me. Grown-ups don't always realize how smart kids are.

I began to cry. "Bingo and Bo Jangles tried to tell me something was happening last night, but I didn't listen. It's all my fault," I sobbed. "I had a fight with my mom. Maybe I hurt her feelings so bad she left."

Mrs. Jones put her arms around my shaking shoulders. "That would never happen, Sophie," she said firmly. "Your mother knows how much you love her. She loves you too much to ever leave you."

When I try to remember everything that happened next, it's all a blur. Within minutes after Mr. Jones called the police, there were squad cars in both driveways. Soon there were clusters of staring neighbors standing on the sidewalk as policemen and private detectives went in and out of our house. Word of Mom's disappearance had spread like wildfire. When a policeman and a policewoman came over, the policeman knelt so he was eye level with me. He was a heavy man with a large stomach and bright blue eyes. He reminded me of a teddy bear.

"When did you last see your mother?" he asked.

"When she came into my room to talk to me last night."

The policewoman didn't seem that nice. She was thin, had mousy brown hair, and a mouth I suspected rarely smiled. "Does your mother go off and leave you very often?"

"No. Not unless she has to go somewhere. Then I stay here with Mr. and Mrs. Jones."

"I understand your dad was home on leave a couple of weeks ago."

"Yes, but he had to go back. Mike took him to the airport."

"Who is Mike?"

"He's Mom's editor."

"Are Mike and your mother good friends?"

"Yes."

"Are they more than good friends?"

"What do you mean?" She and the other cop gave each other a knowing look.

"Mike and Mom work together," I said indignantly.

"Your mom's partner says your mom hasn't been herself lately. He said she hasn't been coming to work. Did your mom and dad have a fight before he left?"

"No, but they were sad."

"They were sad?"

"We are always sad when Dad has to leave."

"Did your mom seem upset by anything lately?" the policeman interjected.

"I don't know," I mumbled, my mind going back to the scene of Mom sitting at the table in the kitchen and crying.

"You don't know?"

The questions seemed to go on forever. During the next few days, different grown-ups would show up and ask the same questions over and over. Many of these questions were about Dad.

"Did your dad and mom get along?"

"They were best friends."

"Did your mom and dad fight?"

At first, I was mystified as to why they kept asking about Dad, but then I realized they thought Dad had done something to Mom. I got mad. "NO, I TOLD YOU. THEY LOVE EACH OTHER. MY DAD WOULD NEVER HURT MY MOM! SOMETHING HAS HAPPENED TO HER, AND YOU'RE NOT HELPING!"

I couldn't understand why they didn't seem to believe me. When I told them about Bingo and Bo Jangles' behavior the night before Mom disappeared, they didn't even take notes.

When a policewoman asked me about my grandparents, I told them Dad was from Montana. His parents died when I was little. When Mom was little, her mother put her in Buckner's Orphanage because she couldn't take care of her. When her mother remarried, Mom was able to leave the orphanage. Mom's mother died a few years ago, so I don't have grandparents. I knew she had a stepsister, but that was all I knew because Mom never talked about her family.

Mom's disappearance was aired on the local television stations and made the front page of the newspaper. Then, a story appeared in a slick magazine that Mom had said was nothing but yellow-street journalism wrapped up in a pretty package. The story made it sound like she had run off, or if she was murdered, she probably deserved it.

The saying that in a crisis, you find out who your friends are is true. Some people looked at me with pity, others with morbid curiosity. I soon realized some of those people who pretended to be interested in me wanted to pump me for information. They loved to feed on scandal. Those play dates and invitations to spend the night became fewer and fewer.

Mr. and Mrs. Jones were furious. "Some people thrive on gossip," Mr. Jones said. "Your mother has helped a lot of people over the years. She doesn't deserve this."

But Mom and Dad both had some wonderful friends. They were furious and banded together. They even pooled their money and offered a substantial reward. That resulted in a lot of fake calls. One of Mom's friends even went to a psychic who said Mom had run off with her hairdresser and was living in Europe. Meanwhile, Mom and Dad's other friends organized search parties. I was amazed at the number of people who showed up wanting to help. Many of them were total strangers. Two of Mom's friends appeared on television. They talked about how kind Mom was and how much she and Dad loved each other "Ray would never leave her daughter," her friend Stephanie said. "Something has happened to her." Turning to the audience, she continued, "If anyone knows anything, please contact us. If someone has kidnapped her, please bring her home. Her family needs her."

But there were no ransom calls, so the idea that Mom had been kidnapped died down. Many of Mom's friends made several calls to the police, demanding that more be done. Some even went to the District Attorney's office. Posters went up all over the city. Every time I saw one of those posters, I wanted to cry.

There were no clues. As time went by, the public lost interest as other stories took center stage. I began to wonder if this would end up being an unsolved mystery like the ones that ended up as the cold case files I'd watched on television.

In the meantime, Mr. Jones asked the Child Protective Services agent if I could stay with them until my father could make other arrangements. She agreed.

One day, Mr. and Mrs. Jones asked me to sit down in the living room. Sitting across from me on the couch, Mr. Jones took my hands. His face was white. Looking over, I noticed that Mrs. Jones was fighting tears. My father was missing. He had been out on patrol in Afghanistan when his helicopter crashed. When the rescue team found the downed helicopter, there was no sign of him. No one knew what had happened.

I couldn't even cry. Instead, I felt numb as I tried to wrap my mind around the fact that I was now an orphan. I had lost my mother, and now my father was gone. I remembered all of Mom's prayers and her love of God. "Why is he doing this to me?" I wondered. "Maybe there is no God."

A few days, later Mr. Jones' cell phone rang. The voice on the other end of the line was so shrill I could hear every word. "I'm Sophie's aunt, and I'm coming to get her. Please have her ready tomorrow afternoon."

"I'm sure she's very nice, Sophie," Mrs. Jones said later. The expression on her face was uncertain. It wouldn't be long before I would learn that Aunt Rose was anything but nice.

Chapter 5

Aunt Rose is not even my real aunt. She's Mom's stepsister. Mom always said if you can't say something nice about someone, don't say anything at all. Aunt Rose has dyed black hair, brown eyes, and wears bright red lipstick and red fingernail polish. With a voice that was shrill and grating, she talked incessantly, I realized now why Mom never talked about Aunt Rose.

When Mr. Jones found out Aunt Rose planned to take both Bo Jangles and Bingo to the pound, he put his foot down. "No need for that Miss Rose," he said firmly. "I'll keep them for the time being. I know how much Sophie loves those pets. Chris does, too."

"Do what you want," she snapped. "I will not have animals tracking dirt on my carpets and destroying my furniture. As for Chris, from what I hear, he's probably dead." Hearing those words, I had a hollow feeling in my stomach, and my heart hurt. With me trailing behind, Aunt Rose headed for the Mercedes in the driveway. Going to a new house, a new school, and living with an aunt and uncle I didn't even know was scary. Knowing I wouldn't have Bo Jangles and Bingo to come home to almost brought me to tears.

As for my father being dead, I hadn't told anyone about the dream I had the night before. It was so vivid that when I woke up, for a few minutes, I thought it was real. In the dream, I found myself in a strange landscape. It was hilly, but everything was brown. As I walked along a rocky ridge, I was calling for my father. Just when I was ready to give up, I saw him on a hill, waving to me. As I clamored up the steep incline, I saw him and an elderly man standing in front of a cave. The man had a beard and was wearing a striped robe. Dad's head was wrapped in bandages. He was leaning on a handmade crutch. Once I reached him, I burst into tears. "Everyone thinks you're dead," I cried.

"I'm alive. Don't worry. This wonderful man saved my life. I'm coming home, and this time I won't leave you."

From the moment I woke up, I knew my dad was alive. He was hurt, but he would come home.

I tried to get along with Aunt Rose. At first, she was nice, almost too nice. But within a couple of days, she changed. Nothing I said or did pleased her. The house was located behind a gated brick wall in a prestigious neighborhood on Inwood Road, a street lined with expensive homes. Aunt Rose's house was huge. Full of what Aunt Rose called collectibles, it seemed more like a museum than a home. It took two maids who came twice a week to clean it. None of them lasted more than a few weeks before Aunt Rose fired them. Everything in the house had to be perfect. If there was a speck of dirt anywhere, or if I ate a cookie in bed, Aunt Rose came unglued. It didn't take long for me to decide I hated the house, and I hated Aunt Rose. I got the impression Uncle Bob was afraid of her. He either didn't answer when she snapped at him, or replied, "Yes, dear, you're right," or "Sorry, dear." When he did try to talk, Aunt Rose interrupted him, often after he had only said a few words.

Mabel was the cook. At first, we barely spoke; although, I would catch her looking at me as if she wanted to offer a word of encouragement.

Aunt Rose refused to let me have my cell phone. "You're far too young," she snapped when I brought the subject up. One day, she told me I was a financial burden and should be grateful she had given me a home. I didn't know what to make of that comment. I only knew it made me feel awful.

As for my new school, I hated it. All the girls in my class were taller than I was, and most of them were stuck up. The worst one was Sue Ellen. She was blonde, and when I first saw her, I thought she was pretty. The longer I knew her, the less attractive she seemed. She pretended to be nice, but it didn't take long to realize she was mean. If she got mad at someone, she would immediately start sending hateful texts. Then, she would go on Facebook and Instagram where she would spread rumors. She was a bully. When she first saw me, she laughed. "Look at that hair, and look how skinny she is," she said to the girls clustered around her. "I wonder what rag bag she crawled out of."

One day, I was looking in my locker when I heard her talking to another girl. She didn't realize I was there and could hear every word she said. "My dad thinks her father hired someone to kill her mom," she said. "Now he's missing. He's probably gone AWOL."

All I remember is seeing a pink haze. When they pulled me off Sue Ellen, she was screaming. I was sitting on top of her and had her long blonde hair wrapped in my fists, beating her head against the concrete floor. "Take it back," I was yelling, oblivious to the growing crowd of excited kids who had gathered around us. As the teacher marched me to the principal's office, I wondered if I would get expelled. If so, I didn't care.

When Aunt Rose arrived, she put on a performance that could have won an Oscar. As we sat in front of the principal's desk, she pulled a handkerchief out of her purse, dabbed her eyes, and reached over and took my hand. "We don't know what to do with Sophie," she said. "She gets so angry. We've given her everything. We are at our wits' end."

Staring at the floor, I gritted my teeth. I knew Aunt Rose only pretended to care about me.

"Obviously Sophie has anger issues," the principal said kindly. "It's understandable after what she's been through. Has she had counseling of any kind?"

"You're right. I've put in several calls. I'm looking for someone with the right credentials," she lied.

"One more incident out of you, young lady, and you're going to be put in a juvenile home," she hissed through clenched teeth after we crossed the parking lot and got into her Mercedes. "You're incorrigible. Every inch a carbon copy of your mother."

"I hope so," I told myself as I stared at her long, red fake nails gripping the steering wheel.

No, I wasn't sorry, even after spending several nights in my room with nothing to read other than my schoolbooks. No TV, no computer, no cell phone, and as far as Aunt Rose was concerned, no dinner. That's where she was wrong. That first night I heard a small tap on the door. When I opened it, there was a tray on the floor loaded with a delicious meal that even included a big slice of chocolate cake. Once I finished eating, I put a note, "Thank you, Mabel," on the empty tray. I then put the tray back outside the door. Within minutes, it had vanished.

I had lost so much weight my clothes hung on me. Every time I was sent to my room without dinner, the trays appeared. I ate every bite. I owed that to Mabel because I knew she was taking a risk. If Aunt Rose found out, she would be fired.

Mabel had a wonderful laugh. She was a force to be reckoned with. She arrived each morning promptly at seven. A tall, black woman, she was the queen of the kitchen. I learned that she was working to put her son through college and had a daughter going to beauty school. She told me that for her first few years working for Aunt Rose and Uncle Bob, she rode the bus, which required two hours and a transfer to get to their house. A year ago, Uncle Bob surprised her at Christmas with a car. "Your Uncle Bob is a good man," she announced. She moved around the kitchen with silent efficiency, preparing meals that Uncle Bob said were fit for a king. Even Aunt Rose grudgingly admitted Mabel was a great cook. She also knew that her friends would compete to hire her if she ever let Mabel go.

A few days after my fight with Sue Ellen, I was sitting alone at a table in the lunchroom eating my lunch when a very tall black girl walked over. Sitting down directly across from me she said, "Hi, my name is Amy. You may not be big, but you're pretty tough." Then she laughed. Her smile was dazzling.

I learned that Amy had been born in Sudan. She and her mother were refugees who lived in a refugee camp before coming to the United States. A wealthy couple sponsored them, and it was due to them that Amy was able to attend this prestigious school. Like me, Amy didn't have any friends. She towered over everyone in the school, even most of the teachers. She was six feet tall. Weeks later, I met her mother. Clad in colorful African clothing, she made a lasting impression. Her soft voice and beautiful smile immediately put me at ease.

Amy and I became friends. Every once in a while, while we were walking together in the hall, I would hear stifled giggles, but for the most part, everyone left us alone. Every time I saw Sue Ellen, she would give me a dirty look before she hurried off in the opposite direction.

One day, I invited Amy to come home with me. We were in my room with our books spread out on the bed when Aunt Rose walked in. After taking one look at Amy, her thin lips turned down into a jagged line of disapproval. "Amy, I think it's time for you to leave," she said, glaring at me with her arms folded across her chest. Without a word, Amy gathered her things and left.

"What do you mean bringing home trash like that!"

"She's not trash. Her name is Amy. She is my friend. Her mother is a Lost Girl from Sudan. She spoke to our social studies class, and her story was amazing. When she was little, soldiers killed her family, and she walked hundreds of miles to get to a refugee camp."

"You need to associate with girls of your own race and class. Do you understand? Don't ever bring someone like that into this house again. She is so black and tall she's frightening. What will the neighbors think?"

"I don't think they are anything like you. Once they got to know her, they'd think she was cool," I replied quietly.

The slap came so fast I couldn't move away. Standing there, staring into my aunt's eyes, I was reminded of a cobra. It hypnotizes its victim. When it strikes, it's too late.

Again, I was sent to solitary confinement, but the meals came, and, as usual, they were delicious. I guess Aunt Rose was so wrapped up in her social life, attending her various clubs, trying to impress and outdo her friends, she didn't notice I was gaining back some of the weight I had lost. But when I looked in the mirror that same image of a girl with wild hair, freckles, and glasses that always seemed to be sliding off her nose, stared back. Her chest was flat as a pancake.

Sometimes I would cry, but I hated to cry because my eyes would swell up, and my skin would get blotchy. I didn't know how much longer

I could take living there. "Please, God, find my mother and father," I prayed. "If you do, I'll never say anything bad about you again, and I will always be good. I promise. I don't care if I stay skinny and flat chested."

As the days went by, I got angry. Maybe Sheila had been right after all. There probably wasn't any such thing as God. One day, I started running down the sidewalk screaming, "I'm an atheist." People who happened to be outside stared at me in amazement.

Aunt Rose insisted that we eat every night in the large, formal dining room. It was during these times that Mabel, moving back and forth from the kitchen to the dining room, would pat me on the shoulder when Aunt Rose wasn't looking. As for Aunt Rose, as usual, she talked on and on. Who got divorced, who was having financial problems, blah, blah, blah. She never seemed to notice that both Uncle Bob and I would just sit there with our eyes glazing over as we tuned her out.

I guess Aunt Rose wasn't the only one who could be mean. Sometimes, I was mean, too. Usually, Uncle Bob read the paper, barely listening to Aunt Rose, but one day he folded the paper, adjusted his wire rimmed spectacles, and looking directly at me, he began asking questions. Hanging my head, I either answered in a monotone or mumbled. He refused to give up. In a kind and patient voice, he kept trying to engage me in conversation. Finally, Aunt Rose lost her temper. "Just shut up, Bob," she said. "I can't believe we are stuck with this dreadful child. She's pathetic."

Uncle Bob's reaction took me totally by surprise. He was no longer the meek, quiet man I was familiar with. Instead, he looked at Aunt Rose sternly and said, "Give the kid a break. Can't you for once show a little compassion? While I'm at it, I'd like to point out that you're drinking too much."

"How dare you," Aunt Rose hissed. Her face was scarlet, and her eyes were blazing.

"It's beginning to show, and people are beginning to notice, so quit complaining about the kid. She's not the problem. You are. Maybe you need to get Dr. Fieldsman to check your medication. On the other hand, why don't you just go shopping. That seems to be what you do best. But for God's sake, leave the kid alone."

Speechless, Aunt Rose got up so abruptly her chair almost fell over. Throwing her napkin on the table, she stomped out of the room. With a small grin of satisfaction, Uncle Bob gave me a wink. Then he picked the paper up and began reading as if nothing had happened. Glancing toward the kitchen, I saw Mabel pass by with a huge smile on her face. From that time on, I was nice to Uncle Bob.

Chapter 6

I have always loved the holidays, especially Christmas. Right before Thanksgiving, I heard voices coming from the front yard. Looking out the window, I saw vans in the driveway. Soon, men were stringing Christmas lights on every bush and tree. Aunt Rose was striding around the yard, waving her arms. "No! No!" I heard her yell at the foreman who looked completely exhausted. "You're missing spots." By the time the day was over, every inch of the yard was sporting decorations, including a Rudolph with a blinking nose, a snowman, and a Santa Claus – all made of plywood and surrounded by the blaze of Christmas lights. That evening, I walked across the street and turned back to look at our yard. Just like the interior of the house, it was overdone.

There also was the overdone Christmas tree. Placed in the foyer, it was decorated by an interior designer. All the lights were white, and the bulbs blue. Silk gold ribbons were artfully wrapped around the branches. It was beautiful, but looking at it, I was sad. I thought about the Christmas trees I had helped decorate at home. There were cardboard ornaments I had made in the first grade along with glass ornaments that were priceless. I couldn't help but wonder what had happened to them.

My spirits began to lift as each day I watched the growing piles of beautifully wrapped packages appearing under the tree. Mabel had taught me how to crochet, so I made her some hot pads. I drew a picture for Uncle Bob and painted a stained-glass ornament for Aunt Rose, knowing she would never use it and would probably throw it away. I drew a picture of Amy and put it in a pretty frame before wrapping it. I gave it to her at school.

A few days before Christmas, I was disappointed when Uncle Bob announced he was going out of town for a few days and would not be with us for Christmas.

On Christmas morning, right after breakfast, Aunt Rose pushed her chair back from the table. "I have a headache, so I'm going to lie down. Mabel has the day off, so help yourself to the leftovers this afternoon when you get hungry. Go ahead and open your presents," she added over her shoulder as she left the room.

Sitting alone under the tree I began opening presents. The biggest box was beautifully wrapped. It was from Aunt Rose. I opened it. Inside the box was lined paper, pens, and of all things, a stuffed orange bear - all obviously bought at the dollar store. The package from Mabel contained a bright pink cashmere wool hat and scarf she had knitted herself. Amy had given me a beautiful small African sculpture. It took me some time before I noticed a small box hidden on the lowest branch. The tag on the box had my name on it. It was from Uncle Bob. It contained a hundred-dollar bill and a small sterling silver dove on a chain. Tears came to my eyes as I thought about him. It was obvious he cared about me.

Three years passed, along with two birthdays. On my first birthday, I woke up excited. "I know today will be special," I told myself. When I came home from school, I found a large, beautifully wrapped box on my bed. Excited, I tore off the ribbon and opened the box. I could only stare in dismay at what was inside. It was the ugliest dress I have ever seen. Red poppies were splashed on a black shiny fabric. It had a Peter Pan collar, rhinestone buttons, and huge puffed sleeves. When I looked closely, it was obvious it was not new. "Great," I thought bitterly. "Now the kids at school will really have something to laugh about." To make matters worse, the dress was two sizes too big. I was tempted to throw it in the garbage but knew that would start a full-scale war. Instead, I put it on a hanger, opened the closet and shoved it as far back as it would go.

Either Aunt Rose was mad because I didn't wear the dress, or she forgot, because my second and third birthdays came and went without her saying a word. Mabel didn't forget. One year she made me a beautiful bracelet. The next year, she made me a necklace. I loved them.

Uncle Bob was out of town on business the day I turned twelve. The first morning he was home, we were sitting at the table eating breakfast, and, as usual, he was reading the paper while drinking his coffee. When I lifted my glass of orange juice, I found, to my amazement, a neatly folded one-hundred-dollar bill had been hidden under the glass. When I looked over at him, he grinned. Not a word was said. I got up, walked around the table, and threw my arms around his neck. His kind eyes and smile almost brought tears to my eyes. As for Aunt Rose, she watched the entire scene with a look of disgust.

One afternoon, I wandered into the living room and saw Aunt Rose sitting on the couch sipping a glass of wine. When I turned to leave, she said, "Don't leave, Sophie. Sit down. Let's talk." I didn't know what to expect. I wondered if I had committed another infraction. Nervously, I perched on the edge of a chair facing the couch.

"Do you have a lot of friends?"

"No," I answered, "just one. It's Amy, and you don't like her."

"Well, don't feel bad. I don't have any friends, either. I have acquaintances but not friends. They are only nice to me because of Bob. I've tried and tried. I've joined the right clubs and have given expensive dinners. I've tried to do all the right things, but nothing has worked. They talk behind my back."

I sat there stunned. Here was the woman I had grown to hate talking to me as if I were her equal.

"I've been snubbed," she continued. "The Dallas Woman's Forum is having a gala, and your uncle and I are not invited. Your uncle says it's because I drink too much. I don't have a drinking problem. I can stop whenever I want to. He doesn't understand that I drink because it helps my nerves. Most of those women drink as much as I do. Just because I spilled a drink on Mrs. Roberts' lap six months ago when we were at an event doesn't make it a cardinal sin."

"Who's Mrs. Roberts?" I asked.

"The bank president's wife, that's who. I think a lot of those women are envious. I have a bigger house and a better wardrobe than a lot of them. The moral of the story is not to trust anyone. If you do, they'll just stab you in the back."

"I'm sorry," I mumbled.

She shook her head and then waved her hand toward the door. "You can go now. I'm sure you have things you should be doing."

Glancing back at her when I reached the door, I realized she had fallen asleep. Slumped on the couch, she was clutching her empty wine glass. Snoring softly, she looked totally dejected. I returned silently, carefully removed the wine glass from her fingers, and sat it on the end table. Spotting a knitted throw, I covered her up and tip-toed out of the room. When I got to my room, I lay down on the bed and tried to wrap my head around the conversation with Aunt Rose. Yes, she drank too much, sometimes to the point where she slurred her words. There were days when nothing pleased her. She complained endlessly. Uncle Bob had talked about her drinking. It seemed like it was apparent to her friends, but she either couldn't or wouldn't admit it. Could it be that under that demanding, complaining facade, was a lonely woman who was actually insecure?

I thought about our house in Lakewood. It was nothing like this mansion. Sometimes there were paw prints on the floors, and sometimes I spilled things. My parents lived well, but they weren't rich like Aunt Rose and Uncle Bob; yet, their lives were filled with happiness and laughter. It was obvious to me and anyone who knew my parents how much they loved each other. I've never seen Uncle Bob and Aunt Rose even hold hands or hug each other. It was almost as if they were resigned to living together in this huge house. I wondered if Aunt Rose had ever truly been happy. I realized I no longer hated her. In fact, I felt sorry for her, but I felt a lot sorrier for Uncle Bob.

That same night I had a nightmare. In the dream, I was standing in front of a large building and staring at an ancient, huge tree. Even though it was nighttime, the dream was in such vivid detail I could even see the veined patterns in each leaf. The canopy of branches and leaves seemed to reach the sky. Animals I had never seen before were pouring out of the tree trunk. As they jumped off the branches, they rushed toward me. Then, the dream shifted. Impossible in the real world, but in the strange nature of dreams, I saw an unusual fish swimming through the air. It was huge. Just before it reached me, it opened its jaws. Horrified, I found myself staring into an enormous gaping mouth that had rows and rows of razor-sharp teeth. I wanted to run, but my feet refused to move. Just as the monster reached me, I woke up. Shaking and covered in perspiration, it took a few minutes to realize I was in bed in the safety of my bedroom. "What a horrible dream," I thought. "I wonder what brought that on?" It was some time before I was able to go back to sleep.

I also was having a recurring dream that wasn't exactly a nightmare. In some ways, it was worse. The settings were different each time, but the dreams were always about my mom. They always ended badly.

In one dream, I was standing in her bedroom watching her brush her long red hair. I was so happy to be with her. For the first time in a long time, I felt safe. Suddenly, she turned to me and said, "Sophie, I have to go. I will probably never see you again."

"Why?" I cried. "Please don't leave. I can't get along without you."

"You told me you hated me," she said sadly. With that, she got up and walked out of the room. Running after her, as I turned the corner of the hallway, I realized she had disappeared. Even though I searched every room, I couldn't find her. I woke up crying.

In another dream, we were laughing and singing as we drove down a country road. Mom suddenly pulled the car over to the side of the road. "I have to leave, Sophie," she said.

"Please, don't go. I promise you I'll be good for the rest of my life."

"You told me you hated me." She then got out of the car and started walking down the road. At first, I couldn't get the car door open. When I finally did, I got out and began chasing her, but no matter how fast I ran, I couldn't catch up. She was far up the road when I saw her turn around a bend. When I reached it, she was gone. Again, I woke up crying.

A few months later, one night I had what, at first, seemed like a repeat of the first dream about my father. Again, I was looking at a strange, desolate landscape. Brown hills were strewn with rocks. Standing just out of reach was my father. As in the first dream, his head was bandaged, and he was leaning on an older, bearded man. "I'm coming for you," he said. When I woke up, I knew he was alive.

The next day was Saturday, and I woke up knowing with certainty that something wonderful was about to happen. I almost danced down the stairs. Since Aunt Rose and Uncle Bob were gone, I went directly to the kitchen where Mabel had already fixed my breakfast.

"You're looking perky this morning, Miss Sophie. "What's got you so excited?"

"I don't know. I just feel like something good is going to happen today. I feel it in my bones."

"Well child, I'm sure you're right. You just lift up your heart to the Lord and thank him for this wonderful day."

I didn't say anything. I loved Mabel and even though I was now an atheist, I didn't want to hurt her feelings.

"Do you know you are special, child?"

"What do you mean?"

"You've always been special. You are one of those they call the Star Children. God chose your parents when he brought you into this world. You have a destiny. These are hard times, but you will get through them. You're an old soul, and you will always be protected."

"But, Mabel, I don't believe in God anymore," I blurted out.

"I know, and that's alright. You will someday, mark my word," she said with a smile. "God believes in you."

Baffled, I couldn't think of anything to say. I walked out of the kitchen thinking about what she had said. Star Child? I had read about those kids. They were brilliant. I was just average. Mabel had to be wrong.

A couple of hours later there was a knock on my bedroom door. To my surprise when I opened it, there stood Uncle Bob with a huge smile on his face. "You've got a phone call, Sophie. You can take it in my office." I ran downstairs, raced into his office, and picked up the phone.

"Hello, sweetheart. How are you?" The voice was weak and shaky, but it was my father. I started to cry.

"I had a dream about you," I sobbed. "I knew you were alive. Where are you?"

"I'm at the military hospital in Houston. They picked me up two days ago and flew me to the hospital."

"What happened?"

"When my helicopter crashed, I suffered a head injury and a broken leg, I managed to hide until I was rescued by an Afghani native who took care of me. That man saved my life. I'm afraid I'm going to be here for a while. How are you doing?"

By this time, I had stopped crying. I was just happy to hear his voice and hoped he'd keep talking, but he sounded weaker by the minute.

"I'm fine Daddy."

"Do you like your new school?"

"Yes, I do. I have lots of friends. I'm having a great time."

I was lying. Even as I spoke the words, I realized my voice sounded high, and my words were running together. When he didn't respond, I decided he was either in too much pain, or maybe he just wanted to believe me.

Word of my dad's rescue spread. Suddenly, Aunt Rose was being nice, and the neighbors smiled and waved when I walked by. Kids in school looked at me in awe. Amy walked about with an air of self-satisfaction. "She knew her dad was alive," she told everyone she met. "She had a dream. She's psychic." I was surprised when kids started greeting me in the halls. At lunchtime, Amy and I were no longer eating alone. Many of the teachers told me how happy they were my dad had been found and was recovering.

Two months later, I heard the front doorbell ring. Racing down the stairs, I threw open the door. There stood my father. Pale and thin, he was leaning forward and clutching a cane. As I threw my arms around him, I'd never been so happy to see anyone in my life. "Pack your suitcase, honey," he said. "I'll visit with your uncle for a few minutes and then we will go pick up your pets."

Uncle Bob appeared and shook my dad's hand. "Congratulations, Chris," he said. "We're so glad you made it. Come on in."

Aunt Rose was quiet while Uncle Bob and my dad talked. I raced upstairs and packed my few belongings. Running downstairs, I rushed into the kitchen and threw my arms around Mabel and gave her a hug. There were tears in her eyes. "I'm going to miss you, child."

"Oh, Mabel, I will miss you, too. I love you."

"Go on now," she said, giving me a little shove. "Get back in there with your daddy."

A short time later, we parked the car in front of Mr. and Mrs. Jones' house. Before we even got to the house, Bingo was racing down the sidewalk to greet me. He whined, jumped up and down, fell over, and showed his belly, only to repeat the same process repeatedly. I think he was so deliriously happy he didn't know what to do. As for Bo Jangles, at first, he sat outside the door staring at me fixedly. Then he walked slowly down the sidewalk. Once he reached me, he sat staring at me for a minute. Finally, he began rubbing his head on my shoes as he purred. It was a happy reunion.

Nothing could equal my happiness at being with my dad, but it didn't take me long to realize he was different. He had lost a lot of weight. He used to walk tall with a jaunty step, but now he limped. That confident air that had always defined him was gone. He looked sad and defeated. "We have to find Mom," I told myself. "That's the only way things will go back to the way they were."

Chapter 7

Two hours later, we pulled into an apartment complex in a gated community. The two-story house I grew up in had been sold. We now lived in a one-bedroom apartment. I didn't care. I was just happy to have my dad back. Dad insisted on sleeping on the couch. The one thing he was willing to talk about was what had happened to Mom's business right after she disappeared. "I never liked that jerk Crankshaw," he told me over dinner. "Your mom was too trusting. Somehow, he convinced her to give him power of attorney. He fired her loyal employees, including the bookkeeper and editor, and brought in his own people. The crowning blow was when he managed to fire your mother. That's why she was so depressed. After her disappearance, he seized all the assets, claiming the company lost money, and he needed to recoup his investment. As far as I know, he never put a dime into the business. He moved fast the minute your mom was reported missing. He sent me a notarized document with your mom's signature. He sold all the equipment, collected the receivables, and closed everything down. I know your mom would never willingly let go of the house. She loved it. When I got his letter, I requested a leave so I could come to come to Dallas and confront Crankshaw, but the next day my copter crashed. Someday, I'll get to the bottom of this, but for now, we have to hang tough."

"I knew Mom was upset about something, and I hoped she would tell you," I said. "I'm glad she finally did. I just wish she would have told you sooner. I don't think she wanted to worry you."

As Dad and I talked, finally the words I had been afraid to speak tumbled out. "Do you think she's dead?"

"I can't accept that. I believe she's alive, and I will find her if it takes the rest of my life."

Dad tried not to admit it, but I know he was worried about money. "This is only temporary," he often said. "It won't take us long to get back on our feet financially."

To start the new magazine, Dad cashed in the back pay he had gotten from the military, sold his new car, and bought the old Jeep. Mom's editor and longtime friend, Mike, gathered what money he could, and together he and Dad launched the travel magazine they named Texas Trails. Within months, Dad and I would find ourselves driving all over Texas. I love it because it means I get to spend a lot of time with my father. I lost him once, and I didn't want to lose him again.

Mike works long hours writing articles and blogs and overseeing production. Dad sells most of the advertising. Our kitchen has been transformed into an office, but Dad is already looking for office space.

Dad even got me my own cell phone. The first thing I did was call Amy. We text each other, and we post things on Instagram. She has a great sense of humor. She cracks me up, but she has problems, too. She has five little sisters, and her father is mean. Her mother never got to go to school in Sudan, so even though she works hard, there's never enough money to go around. Amy must spend a lot of time taking care of her little sisters while her mother works. Even though she loves them, she told me she'd give anything to be a normal teenager.

In some ways, Amy and I are anything but normal. We don't look like normal teenagers. I weigh less than one hundred pounds, and I wear glasses. My curly hair is totally unmanageable. Because I'm small, a lot of times people don't take me seriously. Many don't realize how old I am.

Amy's skin looks like black velvet. She has high cheekbones and a beautiful face. She's six feet tall. She towers over a lot of people, and they often think she's older. Remembering Aunt Rose's reaction to Amy, I wonder if other people sometimes feel the same way about Amy as Aunt Rose did.

"I bet she's going to be a famous model," I decided. "I'll be a famous journalist who will write stories about her and Sudan."

These were my last thoughts before I fell asleep. Again, I was dreaming. This time there were strange scenes with weird looking animals and even dinosaurs. The dream became a nightmare when I found myself face to face with what looked like a female lion with long fangs. As she hissed, I wanted to run, but I could only crawl. "Help me," I screamed as I realized there was no one to help me.

Chapter 8

I woke up with a start. We were still barreling down the highway toward Salado.

"How much longer will it be?" I asked as I yawned and stretched.

"Not long."

"What made you choose this town?"

Dad began filling me in on some of Salado's history. In the olden days, when Native Americans hunted deer and herds of buffalo, Salado was their campground. In the 1860s, W.H. Armstrong, one of the first settlers in the area, built the Stagecoach Inn. First known as Shady Villa, it sat at the crossroads of the Chisholm Trail and Old Military Road, which linked a chain of forts. It was a great stopping place for cattle drives. With porch balconies shaded by ancient trees, a peaceful setting, and an old-world atmosphere, it wasn't long before the Stagecoach Inn became popular with travelers, cattle barons, and soldiers. Some guests didn't have very good reputations. They included the James brothers and Sam Bass, all famous outlaws. "There's even a cave that was used as a hideout for guests who didn't want people to know they were there," Dad said. "We'll never know how many famous and infamous people stayed there because the guest register was stolen in 1944. The hotel is now owned by the Fosters. They're excited about our visit."

Once we arrived, Dad headed for the office to check us in. After putting Bingo on his leash and draping Bo Jangles around my neck, which was his favorite place, I headed for the courtyard. I was amazed when I turned the corner. There stood an ancient tree. "Is it the same tree in the nightmare I had experienced when I still lived with Aunt Rose?" I wondered. The tree in my dream had been dark and forbidding. This tree looked like something out of a fairy tale. Sunlight dappled the leaves as they danced in the breeze. The base of the trunk was the width and depth of a small room. Two of the branches were so heavy, they were supported by iron stakes planted in the ground. The top, an amazing canopy that reached toward the sky, shaded the entire courtyard. "This can't be the same tree," I decided. "It's similarity to the tree in my dream must be a coincidence."

Bingo and Bo Jangles seemed as amazed by the tree as I was. Bingo, usually silly and rowdy, stood totally still with his nose pointed at the tree and his tail extended in a straight line. Bo Jangles, who had jumped off my back, crouched down in the grass and crawled on his belly until he was well under the branches. "Get back here, Bo," I yelled, half expecting him to climb the tree, but it soon became apparent he had no such intention. Instead, he lowered his head on the ground and positioned it between his front paws. It looked almost like he was praying. Staring at the tree, I felt chills run up and down my spine. I heard a noise that sounded like a soft moan. "My imagination is getting the best of me," I told myself.

Is it possible to have two conflicting feelings at the same, exact time? Staring at the tree, I was apprehensive, but I also felt an almost irresistible pull.

Once we got to our rooms, I rushed to unpack because I couldn't wait to go back outside. "Dad, did you see that huge tree in the courtyard?"

"Yes, I asked the clerk about it when he checked us in. He said it was at least six hundred years old. I want you back here in two hours," he added. "The hotel owner is going to join us for dinner."

Summer evenings in Texas are magical. As the hot sun begins to sink beneath the horizon, the heat eases up, and if you listen hard enough, you can almost hear Mother Nature breathe a sigh of relief. When I was a little girl, I thought twilight was when the earth quit spinning on its axis, paused, and then for a few brief seconds, stood still. "It's the best part of the day," Dad used to tell me. "Twilight is when God's critters are getting ready for bed."

Walking Bingo on his leash and carrying Bo Jangles, I walked around the hotel. I went inside and bought some postcards in the gift shop then went back to our room. I washed and dried my hair and put on my new sundress and sandals. The dress was a pretty shade of pink with embroidered daisies around the hem. I love pretty clothes. Dad lets me pick them out. Even though we don't have a lot of money, he insists I buy clothes that are well made. "You get what you pay for," he says. "Cheap things fall apart." When he saw the dress, he smiled. "You have good taste, honey, just like your mother."

Because I had thirty minutes before I needed to head for the dining room, I raced back outside to the tree. With Bingo sitting quietly at my feet and Bo Jangles on my shoulder, I stared upward. When I placed my hand on the trunk, it was hard, as I expected, but then a strange thing happened. The surface under my hand seemed to soften. Within seconds, it felt as if my hand were beginning to sink into the bark. Startled, I jerked my hand back. "This can't be happening," I told myself. As I continued to stare upward through the leaves, the canopy of branches and greenery seemed to go on forever. The attraction I felt for this amazing tree deepened. At first, the only sound I could hear was the rustling of the leaves in the breeze, but then it seemed like the tree was whispering my name.

Slowly it dawned on me that Bingo, Bo Jangles, and I were not alone. I could feel the hairs standing up on the back of my neck. Shocked, I found myself gazing at a tiny creature that had been camouflaged by the leaves. No bigger than my hand, it had pointed ears, a tiny snout, and brown fur. Grasping a branch with tiny fingers adorned with nails, the critter stared back at me with large yellow eyes that seemed ancient, timeless, and intelligent. I'm sure my eyes were huge, and my mouth was hanging open in astonishment. Watching me intently, the creature began making a sound, somewhere between a chirp and a purr, "Chirrup. Chirrup." Without realizing it, I must have moved because in a flash, the tiny critter was gone.

"Bingo, Bo Jangles, did you see that? What do you think it is? A monkey, maybe?" But whoever heard of a monkey with pointed ears. "Maybe it's somebody's pet, or maybe it escaped from the zoo." Just then, I heard my dad calling me. It was time to go in for dinner.

Chapter 9

I had expected dinner to be boring that evening, but I was in for a big surprise. When I walked into the inn's dining room, Dad was already seated at a table positioned in front of a large stone fireplace that took up one wall. Seeing the pleased look on his face when I sat down, I felt the beginning of a blush wash across my cheeks. Maybe I didn't look so bad, after all. Within minutes, a handsome older man accompanied by a pretty woman joined us.

"Mr. Parker, it's great to meet you," the man said, shaking Dad's hand. "My name is Patrick Foster. This is my daughter Charlotte. I'm the owner of the hotel, and Charlotte runs the gift shop. I hope everything's OK with your room."

Looking at Mr. Foster, I instinctively knew he was a nice person, and so was Charlotte.

"The room is fine," Dad said. "This is my daughter Sophie."

"Hello, Sophie," Mr. Foster said. "I have a grandson your age. His name is Presley. It looks like he's about to join us. He just walked in the door."

As I turned, I saw a kid cross the room and head for our table. His hair was brown and long, but it was slicked back close to his head. While a lot of boys our age slouch, Presley's back was ramrod straight. He did not seem at ease as he walked. In fact, he seemed stiff. I was surprised to see he was wearing a suit jacket, white turtleneck knit sweater, slacks, and shiny loafers. He looked like he had just stepped out of a man's fashion magazine - one that featured expensive clothes. "His mother probably buys all of his clothes at Neiman-Marcus in Dallas," I thought. "I bet he's a snob." Pulling out the chair next to me, he sat down. That dress I was so proud of now seemed a little outdated and even a little dingy. I thought of the Cinderella story where Cinderella's rags are transformed into a ball gown. My Cinderella story was in reverse.

"Presley, this is Mr. Parker and his daughter Sophie," his mother said. "Mr. Parker is writing a cover story about the Stagecoach Inn. He and his daughter will be with us for a while. Hopefully, you'll show Sophie around."

Turning in my direction, but not looking me in the eye, he replied, "Absolutely. I'll be more than happy to show our guest around."

"Is this really a kid?" I wondered. "He looks like a kid, but he talks like he's much older. Maybe he's a robot."

When the waitress came to our table and read off some of the house specials, my mouth began to water. When it was Presley's turn to order, it became obvious he was a sophisticated diner. "I'd like a dozen oysters on the half shell, please, and a Roy Rogers," he added politely. "Oh, and today, I think I'll try the trout."

When it was my turn to order, I ditched the standard hamburger and fries, and after a hasty look at the menu, ordered a Shirley Temple. I then decided on a salad and the chicken casserole. Dad ordered a steak. When it arrived, it was browned perfectly. When he cut into it, the inside was pink. After a few bites, I heard Dad sigh with contentment. "This is the best steak I've had in a long time," he said.

"Glad you like it, Chris," Mr. Parker said. "We wouldn't want a bad review."

"I don't think that's going to happen," my dad replied.

"Dad's specialty is macaroni and hot dogs," I interjected. "This casserole is delicious."

"My cooking skills are limited," Dad laughed. "Sophie has had to put up with eating the few things I can cook. My wife Rachael was a fantastic cook." After we had finished eating, Dad asked, "How was your food, Presley?"

"Great. The food is always great here. That's one of the things that makes the Stagecoach Inn so famous."

Charlotte rolled her eyes. "Presley has eaten in fine restaurants all of his life," she said. "When it comes to food, he's spoiled. Presley is quite the pianist," she added. "He's such a hit with the diners I think I'm going to have to put him on our payroll."

I was intrigued. "Really? That's cool," I commented, hoping to somehow make a connection with this stand-offish kid. When he still didn't look at me, I began to get irritated.

"Presley, why don't you play for our guests?" his mother said.

"Yes, Ma'am."

"What a showoff. I can't believe the way he dresses and talks," I thought as Presley marched to the piano and sat down.

"Why don't you go up and join him?" Dad suggested. "You two can get acquainted."

"Not hardly," I thought. I'd decided in the third grade that boys were stupid. When I lived with Aunt Rose, most of the boys in my class were showoffs, but looking at Dad's face, I realized that for the first time in a long time, he looked truly happy and relaxed. I didn't want to spoil the mood, so reluctantly, I walked across the room and sat down on the piano bench next to Presley. Not seeing any sheet music, I expected him to stick to a few popular tunes. He didn't even seem to notice me, but instead, for a few minutes he sat motionless, staring straight ahead. It was as if I wasn't there because he still didn't speak. I resented being ignored. "I don't think he likes me any more than I like him," I decided.

Suddenly, his fingers began moving effortlessly over the keys. To my surprise, he was playing classical pieces that were complicated. Looking around the room, I realized most of diners had stopped eating. Presley could have been on a stage in a concert hall. Totally relaxed, his eyes were closed as his long fingers danced over the keys. The look on his face was rapturous. He wasn't just playing the music; he was living it. Grudgingly, I had to admit his playing was flawless. Looking back at our table, I saw the look of pride on his mother and grandfather's faces. It was obvious to me by the look on Dad's face that he, too, was impressed. Suddenly, seemingly without giving it a thought, Presley switched to ragtime music. The keys seemed to dance under his fingers. Soon, a group of happy adults were standing around the piano. Someone stuck an empty jar on the piano. Within minutes, it was brimming with bills. "I can't believe it," I heard a man say. "That kid looks like he's only twelve or thirteen years old."

I hated to admit it, but I was impressed. "Presley may be stuck up," I told myself, "but when it comes to his skill as a musician, he's the real deal. He has talent."

"Where did you learn to play like that?" I asked when we returned to the table. Ducking his head for a moment, he finally turned and looked at me with a lopsided grin.

"It's something I've always been able to do. It started when my grandfather got me a keyboard for Christmas when I was seven. I immediately sat down and started playing. It's as if my fingers knew what to do. For some reason, I just need to hear a song or composed piece once, and I can play it. From the time I got that keyboard, Mom's made me take lessons. I usually practice four to five hours a day. I'm taking a break right now before school starts."

As Presley talked, I realized he wasn't at all stuck up. "Maybe he's self-conscious and even a little shy," I decided.

Later that evening while I was in our room, Dad was still visiting with Patrick when Presley knocked on the door. Despite the humidity and the summer heat, he was still wearing the suit jacket, silk shirt, and slacks. At first, he just stood in the doorway, looking awkward. The poise he had demonstrated at dinner was gone. His brown hair was no longer slicked back. Instead, his bangs hung down in his eyes, and a cowlick was sticking up at the top of his head. Unlike earlier, nothing about him was intimidating. Better yet, it was obvious he liked animals because Bingo, jumping up and down, greeted him like a long-lost friend. Bo Jangles showed his approval by winding around his legs and purred.

Looking at me, Presley grinned. "I know. I look like a dork."

"No, you look like a rich kid model. I bet your mom drives you to Dallas and buys all your clothes at Neiman-Marcus. Do you always dress like that?"

"It's my mother's idea. She insists on buying my clothes. I hate most of them. Ever since my dad left us, she seems to have forgotten I'm a kid. She's grooming me to be a concert pianist."

Deciding to change the subject, I kept my voice casual. "That's an amazing tree in the courtyard."

"It's amazing alright, but sometimes it can seem a little spooky."

"Well, you might not believe this, but I had a nightmare about that same tree when I was living with Aunt Rose."

Not saying a word, Presley turned pale.

"Oh, boy, I've blown it," I thought. "I bet he thinks I'm crazy."

"Guess what. I had a nightmare about it, too," he confessed.

I was stunned. "Are you sure it was the same tree?"

"Absolutely," he assured me.

"It's probably just a coincidence," I replied. "I guess we both have vivid imaginations."

"I think there's some kind of mystery connected to that tree. I've spent a lot of time just staring at it, trying to figure out if it's trying to tell me something. When I touch the trunk, sometimes I feel like it's breathing," Presley said.

"That's how I felt when I put my hand on the trunk when we first got here. For a minute, I thought my hand was sinking into the bark. By the way, are there any monkeys in the area, or do you know if one has escaped recently?"

"Monkeys?"

"I saw something in the tree late this afternoon before I came to the dining room. It might have been a monkey, but I'm not sure. It had large yellow eyes and brown fur. It also had fingers, but what is really weird is it had pointed ears that stood up. It was so small it could fit in my pocket. It was really cute."

Presley looked baffled. "I haven't seen anything like that."

"I want to find out what it is. I'm going to wait until Dad goes to sleep, and then I'm going to investigate. I know Dad wouldn't want me to go out in the dark, but I'm afraid if I wait until tomorrow, it will be gone."

"Wow!" Presley replied, looking at me with admiration. "You're not like any girl I've ever known."

"Would you like to come with me? It could be fun."

An expression of doubt crossed Presley's face. "I don't know," he said hesitantly.

"Are you afraid?"

"No, but if Mom finds out, she'll get mad. She worries that I'll hurt my hands."

"Don't you play outside with your friends?"

"I don't have many friends," he admitted sadly. "In my spare time, I connect with guys on the computer because we're involved in games, but I haven't met most of them. Before my dad left, he wanted me to try out for football, but Mom had a fit. I'm always playing the piano."

Thinking back to the time I lived with Aunt Rose, I remembered how I didn't have any friends until I met Amy. Looking at the sad expression on Presley's face, I felt a flash of sympathy. "Are you sorry you ever started playing the piano?"

"No. I tried to quit playing last year, but after a couple of months, I missed it so much I started playing again. My mom was so relieved that she's been a lot more receptive to giving me time to do something other than play the piano. It's been so hot lately that usually I just stay inside playing computer games."

"It would be great if we could catch that critter," I said. Trying to hide my disappointment, I added, "But if you think you'll get in trouble, I guess that means you're not coming."

Presley's face was an open book. His first expression was one of indecision. It was followed by one of doubt. What followed was a look of determination. "I'm coming," he said. "You can count on it."

"I hope you're not wearing what you've got on," I replied.

"I bet if I look really hard, I can dig up some jeans and a T-shirt," Presley laughed. "Don't worry. I'll dress for the occasion."

Relieved and a little embarrassed, I laughed, too. We agreed to meet under the tree at eleven that night.

"Wouldn't it be great if we catch it?" I asked excitedly.

"Totally! I'll bring a flashlight."

Sitting on the bed, I realized my first impression of Presley had been totally wrong. He was not stuck up, and he was not a showoff. He was a kid who didn't get much of a chance to be normal. Like me, he had lost a parent. We had a lot in common, and I regretted the fact that I had misjudged him. "Maybe there's a lesson here," I told myself. I realized that was something Mom would say. For a moment, her face appeared in my mind. It was almost as if she were in the room.

When Dad got back, his mood was upbeat. Normally, he insists I go to bed at ten, but tonight he wanted to talk. "Patrick and Charlotte are going to introduce me to a lot of locals," he said. "The history in this area is amazing. Our readers are going to love it."

As he continued talking, I started to get nervous. "It's late, Dad. I'm really tired. It's been a long day. I think I'll go to bed," I said, adding an exaggerated yawn for effect.

"Sorry, sweetheart. You're right. Tomorrow will probably be a busy day. I guess it's time to turn in."

Lying in bed and pretending to be asleep, I could hear him moving around. Finally, he went to bed, but it was a long time before he turned off the light. Looking at the glow of the alarm clock next to my bed, it was already past eleven. Finally, I heard faint snores. Moving across the room, I pulled on my jeans, shirt, and tennis shoes and grabbed the backpack I had filled earlier with items we might need. "Don't make a sound, Bo Jangles," I warned before putting him in the backpack. The last thing I saw before closing it were his two green eyes staring out at me. I attached Bingo's leash, crept across the room, opened the door, and slipped out into the deserted hall. To my relief, the only thing I heard were muted voices coming from one of the rooms and the soft whir of the ice machine. When I got off the elevator, I immediately moved toward the side entrance hoping no one would notice me. Even though it was late, I knew there was a strong chance there would be someone in the lobby, but I wasn't too concerned about that. Even if they noticed me, they were guests. To them, I was just a kid wandering around at night when I should be in bed. I slipped out the side door.

It was a beautiful Texas night. The delicious smell of gardenias wafting through the air was dizzying. It was a dramatic contrast from the sterile air-conditioned environment inside the hotel. A full moon suspended in the starlit sky looked close enough to touch. As I ran across the lawn, the only sound I heard was the insistent hum of cicadas – harmless winged insects that are common in the South. Their shrill singing is just part of the night sounds I have always associated with summer. To my relief, Presley, wearing jeans, was waiting for me.

"I thought you'd never get here," he said. "I was beginning to think you'd lost your nerve."

"Are you kidding? I didn't think my dad would ever go to sleep."

"I know what you mean. I had to crawl out the window."

"Did you bring the flashlight?"

"Sure. I wouldn't forget something like that."

We both slowed down as we approached the tree. It had looked beautiful during the afternoon but was downright scary tonight. Glancing over at Presley, I could see, like me, he was apprehensive. Also like me, I suspected he felt the invisible pull that was drawing us toward the base of the tree.

Once we got there, I stopped for a minute and so did Presley. "Maybe we should wait until tomorrow," I told myself. How easy it would be to go back to the hotel, open the door to my room, and slip into bed. No one would ever be the wiser.

Then I thought about that strange little creature. Because I had seen him earlier, there was a good chance he might still be in the tree.

"Are you with me on this?" I asked. "If you want to go back, I'll understand."

"No, I'm as curious as you are. I've got you. Let's do it."

With that, we both moved forward, never for a minute realizing we were walking into danger. We had no way of knowing we were about to embark on a journey where we would end up so lost that we would find ourselves wondering if we would ever find our way home.

Chapter 10

After standing at the base of the tree for a few minutes and staring up into the branches, Presley and I both began to climb. Bo Jangles, now draped around my neck, was hanging on for dear life. Hearing a small whimper, I realized Bingo was scared. "Don't worry, Bingo. I've got you. Everything is fine," I told him in my most confident voice. I didn't want to admit it, but I was scared, too.

I have climbed a lot of trees in my life, but this one seemed different. I used my arms to reach the branches, but instead of having to hug the tree with my knees, every few inches there were indentations that fit my feet perfectly. I could hear Presley right behind me. When I finally got to the upper part of the tree, I straddled a huge branch, leaned down, and grabbing Presley's hand, pulled him up until he was sitting next to me.

"Wow! This is a lot easier than I thought it would be," Presley said. "It was almost like climbing stairs."

"I bet someone has climbed this tree before us," I responded. "Those indentations had to be put in earlier."

"Have you seen the monkey yet?" Presley asked.

"No, it's too dark. Give me the flashlight."

Moving the flashlight in a wide arc, I didn't see anything at first. I was about to give up when I heard the same soft noise I'd heard earlier in the day. "Chirup. Chirup. Chirup." Pointing the light in the direction of the sound, I saw the same tiny face staring at us intently.

"Look, Presley. There it is!"

"I see it. It's awesome! Do you think we can catch it? Let's take it back to show everyone. If we don't, they'll never believe us."

Because I'm taller than Presley, I stretched out my arms as far as they would reach. I expected the little critter to vanish into the leaves. Instead, he seemed oddly unafraid and continued to stare at me. I leaned forward even further until he was just inches from my fingertips.

"I've almost got it, Presley. Look! It's not even scared."

Presley put his arms around my waist. "I've got you. You can do it." I leaned out even further. Just when I was finally able to wrap my hands around the small furry body, I began to slip. Letting go of the creature, I tried to grab a branch but couldn't reach it. As I fell, my body seemed to hang motionless, almost as if I were floating in air, for the first few moments. I was dimly aware that Bo Jangles was howling as he tried to climb up my back, Bingo was yelping, and Presley was shouting. The sensation of falling was sickening. I realized too late this had not been a good idea. My last thoughts were that Presley and I would die. Presley would never play the piano again, and my dad would end up alone. It was all my fault.

Chapter 11

"Chirup, chirup, chirup." At first, I thought I was dreaming, but I had to be awake because I could feel something poking me in the middle of my back, and I could hear that familiar sound inches from my face. "Chirup, chirup, chirup." For a few minutes, I just lay there with my eyes squeezed shut. When I finally got the courage to open them, I found myself staring into two round, yellow eyes set in a black mask splashed against the background of brown fur. The little monkey-like creature Presley and I had tried to catch was sitting on my chest. I wondered if it had sharp teeth as I nervously watched its little nose quiver. When its tiny fingers began exploring my face, I realized it was just curious. "You're cuter than anything I've ever seen," I told it. "But right now, I need to figure out what is going on."

When I sat up, the little critter slid off my chest and landed on the ground with a thump. The purring sound it had made earlier was now shrill. The expression in its large, yellow eyes was accusing as it stared at me while I sat up. I realized I was getting a good scolding. "Sorry," I said, apologizing, just as I often did with Bingo and Bo Jangles. With that last thought, I jerked myself up into a sitting position.

"Where are Bingo and Bo Jangles?" I wondered frantically. It was then I realized I wasn't wearing my glasses. Turning, I saw the twisted frames lying in the sand a few feet away. Both lenses were shattered. It took a few minutes to process the fact that instead of the usual blur I experienced when I wasn't wearing them, everything was crystal clear. Brilliant colors, sharp lines, and shapes were all in focus. The colors were so vibrant they didn't seem real. With contrasting hues of tans and browns, even the color of the sand was beautiful. I couldn't remember ever seeing anything in such vivid detail, even when I wore my glasses. Just to make sure I wasn't dreaming, I shut my eyes and shook my head. When I opened them, the colors were as vivid as ever.

Hearing a familiar whine, I was delighted to see Bingo and Bo Jangles sitting side by side a few feet away, waiting patiently for me to start moving around just like they did every morning. They knew that once I staggered into the kitchen, they would get their breakfast.

But now, I wasn't in my kitchen. I was on a beach, and I had no earthly idea how I had gotten here. The humidity in the air was so thick it felt like I was in a sauna. Looking up, I saw the sun. Even though the sky was a vivid blue, the sun was a distant ball of yellow light shining through a haze. As I watched, the haze began to fade as the sun moved higher in the sky. "Where am I?" I wondered again.

Cautiously, I moved my arms and legs. I was sore, but nothing seemed broken. Reaching behind me, I rubbed the sore spot on my back, courtesy of the sharp seashell I had landed on. At the same time, I was dimly aware of the usual background noises one hears when they are by the ocean. I heard the cawing of seagulls, the gentle pull of the waves as they surged onto the sand, and the usual clamor of scurrying insects – all sounds that brought back wonderful memories of vacations we had taken when I was a little girl. For a minute, my mind went back to the time when I was seven years old. I remembered sitting on the beach, shoveling sand into a colorful pail. My mother was lounging on a beach chair nearby while my father helped me build a sandcastle. "I was so innocent then," I thought. "I believed those wonderful times with my parents would never end."

Shallow waves were lapping at the sand, inches from my feet. Gazing out at the water, I could see varying shades of turquoise that seemed to go on for miles until they deepened into shades of dark indigo blue. "I must be at the edge of a very shallow sea," I decided. "The water doesn't get deep for miles."

Years ago, Dad had taught me how to read the varying shades of water in the ocean. The lighter the color of turquoise, the shallower the water is. The darker the shade of blue, the deeper the water. Dad said it could be fatal if a ship captain didn't understand how to gauge the different colors of the ocean because there could be shoals of sharp coral, invisible to the naked eye, just inches below the surface. "It's that lack of knowledge that caused many ships to run aground," he told me.

Bewildered, I tried to get my bearings. All I could see were reeds, piles of dead coral, and tangled clumps of dead seaweed.

I noticed that farther down, the shore curved inward. Even at a distance, I could see the water in that inlet was not blue. Unlike the vegetation behind me, there were the roots of mango trees protruding out of the inky surface.

I turned around and looked inland. In the distance, I could see palm trees set in a lush carpet of greenery. As I tried to process what I was see-ing, feeling, and hearing, my brain seemed to be stuck as I tried to wrap my mind around this new reality. Again, I wondered if I were having a dream. If so, it was in Technicolor, complete with smells and sounds. "Maybe I hit my head in that fall and have a concussion," I thought.

The memory of Presley and I, along with Bingo and Bo Jangles, climbing the tree slowly resurfaced in my brain. With a jolt, I remem-bered all of us tumbling head over heels from a branch high up in the tree in the courtyard of the Stagecoach Inn. How did I get here, and where is Presley? That last thought was followed by a horrible possibility. When he fell out of the tree, did he fall into the ocean and drown? The thought of my new friend in the water being sucked under the waves brought tears to my eyes. "Keep it together, Sophie," I told myself as I felt myself start to panic. I knew if I started to cry, I wouldn't be able to stop. Suddenly, a bone-chilling screech split the air. The sound made the hair on the back of my neck stand up as I turned in a circle, staring first at the surrounding brush and trees, then at the sky. Nothing. I wasn't the only one who heard that terrible scream. Bingo was whimpering as he scooted on his belly toward a clump of bushes. As for Bo Jangles, he had vanished. Then I heard another sound. Presley was calling me.

"Sophie, Sophie, where are you?"

When I spotted him racing down the beach toward me, I ran as fast as I could to meet him. A few minutes later, we collided, falling into a tangled heap of legs and arms on the white sand. Clinging to each other for a minute, all we could do was lie there. When I finally pulled away and looked at him, his face was so white his freckles looked like black splotches. His eyes were huge.

"Sophie, are you alright?"

"I'm fine," I mumbled. Then, before I could stop myself, I burst into tears. "I was afraid you had drowned. I don't know where we are or how we got here."

"Don't cry. It's going to be OK." I knew he was just saying that to make me feel better. He was biting his lip, and I realized he was doing everything he could to keep from crying.

I don't know how long we lay there before we realized the sun was making a slow descent toward the horizon. The mist had cleared, and the sky was slowly being transformed into a canvas that would be the background for a spectacular sunset splashed in hues of gold, pink, violet, and magenta. I knew it would be followed by darkness. Remembering that terrible scream I had heard earlier, I shivered. We should not be out in the open. Something was out there, and it was big. If it was like a lot of predators, it hunted at night, and more than likely, it would be looking for a meal. Nighttime was a few hours away, so we needed to get busy.

"I'm hungry," Presley announced, looking at me with his lopsided grin. I was pretty sure he had heard the same thing I had heard earlier, and like me, he didn't want to talk about it. I accepted the fact that this was not a dream. It was getting cold, and I felt a chill all the way to my bones.

Presley was amazing. I already knew he was a gifted pianist and whiz-kid, but he also had some awesome Boy Scout skills, which he demonstrated as he shifted into high gear. Not only had he brought a flashlight for our adventure, he also had brought a jackknife. After carefully gathering some twigs and dried seaweed, he fashioned a stick with one end anchored in a small hole he had carved in a flat piece of weathered wood. Spinning it between his palms, it wasn't long before his efforts produced sparks. I rushed back and forth along the beach gathering driftwood while Presley shielded the small flame with his hands. A short time later, we had a blazing fire. Then, pulling large pieces of brush and wood away from the beach, we built a shelter of sorts. Even though it wasn't big enough inside for us to stand up, there was room for both of us to sit up and lie down. From the outside, it looked like a pile of weeds, sticks, and brush. For the time being, this would be our new home.

"What do you think we should do about food?" I asked.

"I guess we'll have to figure that out tomorrow,"

I gazed at the water and tried to ignore the growls coming from my stomach. It still wasn't dark, and the water looked inviting. "Should we at least get our feet wet?" I suggested.

"Good idea. We need a break."

Within minutes, we were wading near a reef that was just inches below the surface of the water. Feeling large lumps under my toes, I reached down and probed the sand with my fingers. It wasn't long before I pulled up a large, gray, bumpy shell. It was the biggest oyster shell I have ever seen. Holding it high in the air, I yelled, "Look, Presley! I've found an oyster bed. They're huge!"

Presley was grinning from ear to ear. "Looks like we'll have dinner after all." Bingo and Bo Jangles seemed to agree because Bingo was barking, and Bo Jangles was meowing as they pranced up and down the beach, waiting for us to return after we gathered the oysters.

As a little kid, I had dug for clams and oysters. It took a lot to make a meal. These oysters were as big as dinner plates. To my delight, when I started prying them open with Presley's knife, many of them contained pearls. Unlike the perfectly matched white pearls Mom wore, these were the size of marbles, and many of them weren't white. Instead, they ranged in iridescent shades of blue, pink, and gray. Nature's perfection at its best, each one seemed to glow.

At the moment, we and the pets were hungry. After carefully picking out the pearls, I placed the open shells carefully on the coals where the flames of our fire had died down. Within minutes, they were sizzling.

Using two flat sticks, I carefully lifted each one off the coals and placed them on a plank that was on the ground. I knew that Bingo would eat anything, so I wasn't surprised when he immediately gulped one down. Bo Jangles was another matter. A finicky eater at home, he had made it clear from the time he was a small kitten that he wouldn't eat anything that didn't contain shrimp. Fancy Feast cat food had been a staple on our grocery list. To my amazement, he pulled one of the oysters off the plank, placed it between his paws, and started eating. Soon, all of us were eating. "This is like a family meal," I thought. "The only thing missing is the dining room table and our parents."

I turned my attention to the pearls. "A girl can't have too much jewelry," Mom used to tell me with a laugh. As a little girl, I had spent hours going through her jewelry box trying on rings, necklaces, earrings, and bracelets, daydreaming of the day I would be big enough to wear them. The one thing Mom wore almost every day, was a pair of earrings Dad had given her on their first anniversary. Each pearl was centered in a circle of diamonds and set in gold. Her initials were engraved on the back. Mom loved those earrings so much she wore them with almost everything, whether it was a business suit or a pair of jeans. She some-times even wore them to bed.

"I'm going to gather a whole bunch," I decided after selecting one large pearl and dropping it in my pocket. "When I get home, I'm going to put them in a pretty box, tie a ribbon around it, and give it to Mom when we find her."

It took a few minutes to find a piece of driftwood that had a hollow core. Placing the pearls in the hollow end, I stuck it in the sand, leaving it in an upright position under a nearby bush.

Next, we gathered large, green leaves. Hoping for rain, we folded them into the shape of shallow bowls, which we then anchored with pieces of driftwood. Even though we were kids, we knew no one could last very long without water.

By this time, I had named my furry little friend Gizmo. To my surprise, he, Bingo, and Bo Jangles became friends. When he wasn't running his tiny fingers through my hair, he would perch himself on

Bingo's back and ride him as if he were his own private pony. More times than I could count, he would torment Bo Jangles by pulling his tail. Bo Jangles was a skilled hunter who had often brought us presents of dead mice and even snakes. I was surprised that he tolerated Gizmo's teasing. I decided he thought Gizmo was a kitten, and he was too much of a gentleman to spank a naughty kid.

Because I had given up on God, I had not prayed in a long time, but that first night, when we all crawled into our crude shelter, I offered up the most desperate prayer I had ever said. "God, I am sorry I said I was an atheist. I hope that didn't hurt your feelings or make you mad. If you are real and hear this prayer, please help us to get home. If you do, I promise I'll be good the rest of my life."

Then, with Presley next to me, Bingo and Bo Jangles curled up at my side, and Gizmo tucked under my chin, I fell into a deep, dreamless sleep.

Chapter 12

The next morning, it rained, filling our leaf bowls with water. Going through my backpack, I found two Hershey bars. When I gave one to Presley, you would have thought it was Christmas. Breaking off each square of chocolate, I tried to make it last as long as possible. Never had chocolate tasted so delicious, but as each piece melted in my mouth, I was reminded of home.

Sometime later, we both noticed what looked like a cloud floating just below the surface of the water near the shore. When it got closer, we realized it was a huge clump of worms. "It's larva," Presley announced. "Let's go fishing." Within minutes, we had scooped a handful of the larva out of the water and dropped it into one of the leaves that was still filled with water. In my backpack, I found some string, along with a couple of safety pins. After attaching the string to a pole, we each placed a worm on the improvised hooks and threw out our lines. No sooner did they hit the water than we each caught a fish.

Everything was going well until there was a huge splash as a large fish jumped out of the water just inches from my line. With its large, black body and what appeared to be wings, it had a head shaped like a snake. When it opened its mouth, I was shocked to see rows and rows of razor-sharp pointed teeth. My mind immediately went back to the night-mare I had experienced when I lived with Uncle Bob and Aunt Rose. The fish in my dream was now a reality. Not only was this world strange, it was dangerous. At the time, we had no idea how dangerous it was.

"I guess we won't be doing much swimming," I told Presley.

"We need to stay in the shallow water. The water is so clear we should be safe as long as we're careful."

For the next couple of days, we fished, ate oysters along with our catch, and swam in the shallow water. We also spent a lot of time staring out across the bay hoping to see a boat – any boat that would not only promise the possibility of rescue but would prove we were still existing in the world we had come from. No matter how hard we looked, there was never a boat. One day, as we gazed out as far as we could to the horizon, where the water was the deepest navy blue, we saw a huge shadow of an enormous fish gliding along just below the surface.

"Must be a whale," I said.

"Yep."

We were shocked one evening to find crabs crawling near our campsite on the beach. These were not the crabs so common in the world we had come from. They were enormous. Some of them were five- or six-feet wide with pincers that were at least a foot in diameter. We both knew without speaking that these creatures could be dangerous. No more wandering around the beach in the dark.

It was early the next morning when I heard a high-pitched scream. It was Bingo. Instead of his usual bark, his high-pitched cries sounded almost human. Rushing out of our hut, we were horrified to see he was caught in the claw of a huge crab that was making a sideways crawl and scurrying rapidly toward the water. Acting instinctively, Presley and I grabbed two long, heavy sticks that were lying on the ground and rushed toward the crab. Presley got in front of the giant creature, blocking its path. I started hitting its body from the rear as Presley aimed for its head. Rearing up on its back legs, the crab went into a defense mode, but in so doing, it dropped Bingo, who crawled away whimpering. Clacking its claws, the agitated crab lunged at us. We did not back down. We knew we had to win this battle, not only for our sakes but for Bingo and Bo Jangles as well. The battle seemed to go on forever before we managed to kill the crab.

As I rushed over and picked up Bingo, Gizmo climbed up my leg and sat on my shoulder, peering down at Bingo with a look of concern in his large, gold eyes. As I cradled Bingo like a baby, his little body was limp at first, but then to my relief, he lifted his head and licked my hand. Even though he was shaken up, he was unhurt. I almost started to cry. A little later, Bingo had recovered enough so that I could put him on the ground. Gizmo, instead of tormenting him as he usually did, sat motionless between his paws.

"I can't believe this happened," I told Presley.

"Right. We need to make sure Bingo and Bo Jangles don't go out of our shelter in the morning before we do."

Staring at the body of the crab, an idea began to form in my mind. "Presley, I bet if we cook that crab, it will be delicious."

"Absolutely," Presley replied with a smile. "We used to boil the crabs we caught on the beach."

"We'll do the same," I replied, thinking back to a survival show I had seen on television.

We dug a very large pit in the sand and lined it with several layers of large palm leaves. Carefully, we placed hot coals on a plank, which we then placed in the bottom of the pit. It took several trips to fill the hole with water. Due to the hot coals, within minutes, the water was boiling. Because of its size, it took both of us to push the body of the crab to the side of our homemade pot and shove it over the rim into the hot water. It wasn't long before the shell of the crab was bright red. When we decided it was cooked, we used all our strength and large sticks as levers, managing to lift the crab out of the water. We then placed it on a large, flat rock and waited for it to cool.

Once we cracked open the shell, we each took a tentative bite. Presley looked at me and grinned. "This is freaking delicious," he announced.

"Minus the butter," I laughed.

Because of the crab's size, there was more than enough to feed all of us. In fact, we had a large amount left over. Since we had dug the hole so deep, I knew the sand at the bottom would be cool.

"We've created our own ice box," I said.

"Right," Presley responded, "minus the ice."

When we were finished eating, we took the leaves out of the hole to allow the water to drain. We then covered the bottom with rocks, wrapped the leftovers in large leaves, and placed them in the hole. After covering the hole with a large piece of driftwood, we then covered it with sand and planted an upright pole over the pit to mark the spot so we would not forget where it was.

All of us, including Bingo and Bo Jangles, enjoyed the leftover crab meat for two days. I could see Bingo licking his chops as I placed his share on his board. "I wonder if he knows he's eating the adversary who wanted to eat him," I laughed.

"I never thought much about that old jungle law, eat or be eaten." Presley said. "It's never been clearer to me than it is now."

Chapter 13

One afternoon, we decided to explore the area around the mangrove trees. Once we arrived, the trees seemed hidden in the shadows despite the bright sun overhead. Shallow water covered a large stretch of land dotted by roots of trees that resembled skeletal fingers pointing at the sky. This made the scene even spookier than it was. Unlike the fresh, clean smell of the beach, there was an odor that hinted of rotten eggs.

Exploring further, we found ourselves in a tunnel of sorts. Towering mangrove trees had branches that met and tangled overhead. Some of the trees were generously sprinkled with flowers that looked like pink powder puffs. I was tempted to pick one until I realized there were dead fish floating belly up around the base of many of the trees.

"I think the bark and maybe even the leaves are poisonous," Presley said.

Presley and I had brought our walking sticks, so we slowly started moving along a trail. Trying to keep my feet out of the mud, I spotted what appeared to be dry sand covered by dead grass. Jumping, I landed well away from the mire. Glad that I had managed to make the jump without getting my feet wet, it took a minute for my mind to register the fact that I was sinking. What had looked like dry sand, wasn't. Panicked, I tried to lift my feet, but the more I struggled, the faster I began to sink.

"Stand still," Presley yelled. "Don't move! You're in black tar. It's quicksand."

"What can I do?" I responded, trying to keep the panic out of my voice.

"Throw me your stick."

Presley lay on his stomach in the middle of the muddy trail and extended both sticks toward me. Carefully, trying to keep my lower body as still as possible, I leaned forward and grabbed the ends. Pulling as hard as he could, Presley's face was red with exertion.

"It's not working, Presley," I cried.

"Don't give up. Move your hands forward on the sticks and keep your legs still. Whatever you do, don't let go."

I did as he instructed. What seemed like hours later but was probably a matter of minutes, I heard a sucking sound as my feet began their slow ascent back to the surface. By this time, Presley was exhausted, but he kept pulling. I used my elbows for leverage, moving inch by inch over the surface until my body was free. Lying on the path exhausted, it took both of us a few minutes to catch our breaths. Looking back, we spotted a huge skull sticking up out of the tar. Apparently, when Presley pulled me out of the pit, the disturbance in the tar pushed the skull upward making it rise to the surface. "What kind of animal do you think that was?" I asked Presley.

"Whatever it was, it was big. I bet there are a lot of bones in that tar pit, Animals must have come here and stepped on that dead grass just like you did. This tar pit is a graveyard. Let's go back to the beach."

"Yes. I don't want to come here again."

Moving carefully, making sure our feet stayed on the trail, even in the muddy areas, we breathed a sigh of relief when we found ourselves back on the white sand of the beach. Even though we were both filthy, we were too tired to care.

We waded into the shallow water after we were rested and sat down. Looking at the pieces of tar clinging to my legs, I knew getting it all off was going to be a chore. "I'd give anything for a bar of soap," I thought. The cool water lapping gently over my skin felt wonderful as I leaned back. Finally, I sat up and lifted handfuls of sand to begin scrubbing my legs.

Each day, it became more and more obvious that this strange place was dangerous. I suspected that Presley, like me, was wondering what would happen next. We had already found out that danger could be unexpected and come out of nowhere. In the coming days, we would find ourselves facing several dangers. We had no way of knowing then that the worst was yet to come.

Chapter 14

We grew tired of being at the beach, tired of eating oysters and fish, but more than anything, we grew tired of staring out at the horizon hoping to see a boat of any kind that would come and rescue us. I was losing hope, and even though Presley didn't say so, I think he was losing hope, too.

"Look at those palm trees," Presley said one morning as he stared at the green landscape behind us. "I bet there are coconuts on them. There could even be some of them lying on the ground. If not, we can climb the trees and knock some down."

Carrying our sticks, we hiked to the forest. When we reached the palm trees, just as Presley predicted, there were a few coconuts lying underneath the trees. As we looked up, we could see clusters hanging at the tops. We climbed two trees. After a few good shakes, the ripe coconuts fell to the ground. We filled the edges of our shirts with coconuts and carried them back to the beach. Placing each one on a flat rock, we broke it open with a rock. The juice was delicious. Then, using a shell, we scraped out the white flesh. I couldn't remember anything tasting so good.

We returned to the jungle daily, each time venturing a little farther into the interior. The landscape was ethereal. Strands of moss and orchid vines hung from the trees. Although some of the orchids were like the ones I'd seen in grocery stores, others were totally different. The blooms were huge and had vivid color.

The sounds created by a variety of insects, small animals, and brightly colored birds were deafening at times. Flying insects defied belief in size and color. Amazing butterflies swooped around us. Their colors and patterns were so brilliant they dazzled our eyes. The dragonflies were unlike anything we had ever seen. With wingspans of eighteen or more inches, they were stunning.

At a certain time of day, we could detect pulsating lights that seemed to surround all the plants, flowers, and trees. Everything seemed wonderfully alive. Moving through this strange world, it was as if I had stumbled into a science-fiction movie where everything was bigger and brighter than in the world we had come from.

I'll never forget the minute we first discovered the waterfall. Long before we reached it, we could hear the soft roar of falling water that was like a magnet pulling us forward. A short time later, we stepped into a clearing at the base of a huge rocky formation. Sunlight shining through the canopy of branches overhead created a shimmering rainbow reflected in the wide ribbon of water that spilled over the edge of an overhanging cliff before cascading into an inviting pond adorned by floating water lilies.

For a minute, we just stood there awestruck. Then, screaming with delight, we ran forward and jumped in. The feeling of the cool water on my skin felt wonderful as I swam under the waterfall. As the sand and grime washed away, I finally felt clean in what seemed like forever. "No more worrying about not having enough water," I thought happily. I then remembered soaking in those long bubble baths at home. Closing my eyes, I could almost smell the lavender bath oil that scented the water in our over-sized porcelain tub. With my eyes still closed, I thought about the soft white, fluffy towels I used to dry off. As beautiful as this place was, I'd rather be home.

In the following days, when the tide went out, we walked along an exposed sand bar that extended far out into the sea and collected seashells. Ranging in a variety of shapes, colors, and sizes, they were the most beautiful seashells I have ever seen. I marveled at each one's perfection. Too beautiful to discard, I gathered them up, stacking the bigger ones at the bottom of the pile and the smaller ones on top, never realizing that someday they would come in handy.

As each day passed, the memories of the reality we had left behind began to blur. I no longer tried to smooth my hair when I woke up. Sand caked my clothing. The only path to cleanliness was the freshwater pool we visited daily.

We also improved our living quarters. We created what would serve as a roof by weaving large plant leaves we found in the jungle. We then dug our sleeping pit even deeper. The next step was to plant tall bamboo sticks protruding three feet above the pit. After that, we placed bamboo sticks across the top of the protruding sticks, creating a framework for our ceiling. Carefully laying the woven fronds across the framework, we secured everything with the twine we had made by tearing palm leaves into narrow strips. When we were finished, I stood looking at our entrance. I still didn't feel safe. The fact that a lot of predatory animals hunted at night had never left my mind. The realization we were dealing with unknown animals, some huge, made me even more uneasy. "What can we do to keep animals away from our den?" I asked Presley.

Thinking for a minute, he said, "We have to create a brush barrier that no animal would want to deal with."

I sat down next to him and watched him draw designs in the sand. "I guess the next thing we need to do is make a rope," I said.

We had found a lot of uses for the palm fronds. They could be torn into vertical pieces and could be woven into mats. Incredibly strong once they were woven, they were impossible to break. It was obvious the pieces were perfect for what we needed. We began cutting the fronds, slitting them into strands and braiding them. It wasn't long before we had a long rope. To test it, we pulled on it, ran it up and down jagged rocks, and did everything we could to make it fall apart, but it didn't break.

"We have to go back to the swamp," Presley told me with a serious look on his face.

"Oh no!" Just the thought of that area gave me the creeps.

"Don't worry. We'll be careful. I saw some bushes there that had thorns on them. We'll cut several branches and build a barrier we can move across the entrance before we go to bed. We can leave it lying on the ground outside during the day."

That's exactly what we did. We headed back to the swamp, and this time I stayed on the path knowing there were hidden tar pits just waiting for me and other living things to wander onto the dead grass.

When we reached the thorned bushes, we carefully cut several of them into long lengths. "How can we get these back to our camp?" I asked Presley. "Those thorns are awful. I've already cut myself a couple of times."

Presley pulled a ball of our homemade twine out of his pocket. We carefully laced the canes together, trying not to cut ourselves. We may as well have not bothered being careful because by the time we were done, our hands and our arms were covered with scratches. Then, using our rope, we attached it to the barrier, which we pulled back to our camp. After placing it at the entrance, we stood back a few feet to examine it. It looked like a heavy brush of thorns that would discourage almost any wild animal. "Presley, that is amazing," I said. "Your design is so good there is no way anyone could tell it's a hidden room."

"You helped," Presley said. "I couldn't have done it without you."

A little later, I noticed Presley staring at his hands.

"Are your hands OK?"

Watching him, I realized he was thrilled. He held them up for my inspection. His long fingers were covered with scratches, and there were callouses on his hands. "My mom will have a fit if she ever sees this," he laughed.

We placed the barrier at the entrance at night and removed it in the morning. It became part of our routine and gave both of us an added sense of security.

One day, as Presley and I were gorging on oysters and berries, I happened to look up. With berry juice staining his chin and dirt in his hair, Presley was a wreck. I started to laugh. "What's so funny?" he demanded. Seeing the look on my face, he grabbed the end of his soiled shirt and made a half-hearted attempt to wipe his face.

What had seemed so funny moments ago was horrifying as I realized

I probably looked as bad, if not worse. I thought back with yearning to the large, tiled bathroom in my house in Lakewood. I remembered how, with a flick of the wrist, hot water was at my fingertips. How many times had I, without even thinking, absent mindedly turned on an electric light? I had taken everything for granted. I thought back to the time I had read *Lord of the Flies*. I knew the story line well. Little boys lost in a jungle gradually turned into savages. Would we turn into savages, too? Mom had said that civilization was not just built on education and money; it was built on character, customs, and manners. Glancing over at the pile of seashells, an idea began to form in my mind.

"Presley, we've got to get our act together. Just because we're lost doesn't mean we have to live like animals."

Obviously puzzled, he just stared at me.

I remembered how Mom, who was a great cook, set the table. The way that table looked at mealtime somehow added to the taste of the food, making it even more delicious. I decided we needed to remember our table manners. I had hosted a lot of tea parties in the treehouse in our back yard in Dallas. I learned early on that those who came were little girls like myself. The boys in our neighborhood would die before they would get caught "playing house."

When Presley realized what I had in mind, he was reluctant at first, but before long, he was carving pieces of wood with his pocketknife, creating knives, forks, and spoons. Those seashells we had collected would serve as plates and bowls. A large, flat-surfaced rock became our table, and like a lot of kitchen tables, it served many purposes. Every day, late in the afternoon, we would clear the surface and place large leaves under flat seashells that served as plates. We gathered moss we found hanging from trees in the forest and shaped it to cradle shells shaped like bowls. Hollowed out coconut shells became cups for the delicious coconut milk we collected daily. In the center of our makeshift table, I placed flowers I had picked earlier. Once the table was set, I would stand back and look at it with satisfaction. "Mom would be proud of me," I thought wistfully.

Flowers grew everywhere. There were too many varieties to count. The bees hanging around the flowers were huge. I loved watching them drink the nectar because sometimes, after feeding, they fell to the ground as if they were drunk. After a few minutes, they would stagger up and fly off to the next flower.

The colors of these flowers ranged from pastels to vivid shades so intense they didn't look real. The flowers defied reality. The minute I picked a flower, a bud would reappear and bloom, an exact duplicate of the one I had just picked and held in my hand. The first time this happened I thought I was hallucinating. Sometimes I would stand for hours transfixed by the flowers that reappeared as if by magic. I knew that hothouse flowers grew back fast in the world we had come from but not at the speed these flowers did in this strange world.

Presley and I grew more careful about our appearance. I found a shell with long spines and carefully began working it through my hair. The first time there was so much gunk in my hair, it was almost impossible to comb. Presley did the same. I was too kind to comment on the fact that no matter how hard he tried, there was no way he could control the cowlick on the top of his head. Each day, we would dive into the pool where we would spend hours. We would scrub ourselves with sand, wash our clothes by pounding them on rocks, and spread them out on bushes to dry.

One day, I happened to look up while swimming under the water-fall. At first, I thought I was looking at a large shadow, but upon looking closer, I realized it was a cave. "Look, Presley. Swim over here. You won't believe what I've discovered."

Presley was as surprised as I was. "That looks like it could provide shelter if we ever needed it," he said. "It might come in handy one day."

"But how can we get to it?"

"See those jutting rocks on the side? I think they lead right down into the water."

No matter how deep we went into the jungle, without saying a word, Presley and I would head back to the beach every day. We didn't want to wander so far from where we landed that we couldn't get back. We were still clinging to the hope that somehow, some day, we would be rescued.

In the late afternoons, we would build a fire and snack on nuts, fruit, and berries we had found in the jungle. Some of the fruit was unlike anything I had seen back home, and at first, we were afraid to try it in case it was poisonous. Carefully, we would take a small bite, chew it, then spit it out, waiting to see if we had a bad reaction. But never once did we experience cramps or vomiting. Each piece of fruit was beyond delicious.

"No candy, no sodas, no potato chips, or processed sugar," I thought. "I'm probably eating better than I've ever eaten in my life. Mom would be delighted."

During the day, I tried to push thoughts of home and my dad and mom out of my mind. I think Presley did, too. But every night when the sun went down, both of us would get quiet. "I know my dad is worried," I told Presley one night.

"My mom and grandparents are worried, too," Presley said. "I'm sure they are frantic. I just wish there was a way I could let them know we're OK."

"What about your dad?"

"We haven't heard from him in a long time. I'm not the kid he envisioned. Because I'm a boy, he expected me to be an athlete. I think he's disappointed in me."

"How can that be?" I said incredulously. "You're a brilliant pianist, and you're smart."

"He never came to one of my performances," Presley said sadly. "I don't think he even cares."

I wanted to say something that would make Presley feel better, but I couldn't find the words. Even though Mom was missing, I knew without a shadow of a doubt that both my parents loved me. How awful to have a parent who didn't. I realized that despite everything, I was lucky. Fighting back tears, I looked at Presley. He was fighting back tears, too.

No matter how hard I tried to convince myself that I was having a great time, there was an aching hole in my heart. I wondered what Amy was doing. Did she think I'd forgotten her? I even missed the Texas heat. Most of all, I missed my dad.

At night we went into our shelter followed by Bo Jangles, Bingo and Gizmo. This was the time of day that was the hardest. I think Bo Jangles and Bingo knew we were sad. Even Gizmo seemed to sense something was wrong. He would sit on my chest and stare into my eyes with a quizzical look on his face. "Why are you sad?" he seemed to ask. Bo Jangles would lay against my back and purr. Bingo somehow managed to sleep on his back, often taking up too much room. During the night, I would feel his cold nose on my face as he patted me with a paw. I never wanted Presley to know I was crying, and I never complained, but sometimes I would wake up and feel his shoulder shaking next to mine. I knew he was crying, too.

Chapter 15

The thought of the cave behind the waterfall was always in the back of our minds. One day, Presley looked at me with that familiar grin on his face. "Let's grab our rope," he said. "I'm dying to see what's in that cave."

"Me too," I replied happily.

The night before we decided to explore the cave, Presley selected a clam shell that had both sides attached. He gathered dry moss and weeds and made a nest inside the shell. The next morning, we selected two thick branches that we cut into three-foot lengths. We wrapped the ends in dry moss and tied them with thin strands of fronds, creating a thick wad of dried material. These sticks would serve as torches. After Presley carefully put a couple of live coals in the shell, we started out. Within a short time, we reached the waterfall.

Presley was right about the rocks that could be climbed to reach the cave. Bushes jutted out at intervals. "If one of us slips, hopefully we can grab a branch," I thought. To be on the safe side, we tied each end of the rope around our waists and made our way up the rocks to the ledge that led us behind the waterfall. The mouth of the cave was large. Lighting our torches, we slowly moved inside, hoping we wouldn't find ourselves face to face with a strange animal.

"Wow, this is neat," Presley said.

"Let's see where it leads. Maybe there's an exit."

We made our way deeper into the cavern. Before long, the passage narrowed into a tunnel, making it difficult to hold our torches and continue. Crouching down, we managed to move forward. Minutes later, we found ourselves in an enormous room. At first, all we could do was stare as we moved our torches in a wide arc. Pillars of crystal rose from the floor and hung from the ceiling. The light from our torches was reflected in the crystals, creating a multitude of colored lights. To this day, I have never seen anything so beautiful.

"This is amazing," Presley said. "There are a lot of caves in Texas that have stalagmites and stalactites, but I've never seen anything like this."

"Stalagmites and stalactites? What is the difference?"

"Stalagmites rise from the floor. Stalactites hang from the ceiling. We shouldn't touch anything. The oil from our hands can cause damage."

When we spotted a chamber behind one of the largest stalagmites, we decided to investigate. Once we entered, I didn't notice anything at first. Then, I saw a small moving object fall from the ceiling and land inches from my feet. It was a bat. Before I had time to react, a slithering form sped across the floor, grabbed the bat in its mouth, and vanished into the shadows. Dropping my torch, I screamed. "What was that?"

"A coach snake," Presley said cheerfully as he reached down and retrieved my torch.

As I looked up, I realized there were millions of bats hanging from the ceiling. "Yikes," I said in a quavering voice. "Don't bats suck your blood?"

"Vampire bats do," Presley said, "but these bats don't look like vampire bats. They're harmless and do a lot of good because they eat insects. They swarm out at night to hunt."

Embarrassed, I did not want Presley to know that when it came to creepy-crawly things, I was a coward. As I moved my torch lower, I spotted a dark shadow on a rock. Looking closer, I realized it was a huge, hairy spider.

"Yikes. Let's get out of here."

"It won't bite you," Presley laughed. "It's a cave wolf spider. It's blind. It doesn't have eyes."

Apprehensive but curious, I looked closer, but at the same time, I tried to keep my distance. The spider stayed motionless. Presley was right. It had blank areas where the eyes should be. "Does it build webs?" I asked.

"No, it survives by sensing movement and scent."

Regardless of Presley's lack of fear, I began walking rapidly back toward the tunnel. "How come you know so much about this stuff?" I asked.

"When I was little, I used to collect bugs, and I was fascinated by snakes," Presley laughed. "My mother believes the only good snake is a dead snake, and that goes for insects and bats, too. One day, a friend and I found two garter snakes. Mom was recovering from an illness, so she was in bed watching television. We were so excited about what we found we rushed into her room and threw the snakes on her bed, thinking she'd be excited, too. She was excited but not in the way we'd hoped for. She hit the ground running and ran right out of the house."

Seeing the image in my mind of Presley's mother Charlotte, usually so well-groomed and without a hair out of place, running outside in her pajamas, I laughed. "What did she do after that?"

"She sat us down and sternly made us promise to never bring snakes, bats, rats, mice, or bugs into the house again. I guess she understood that little boys have an entirely different outlook on life when it comes to nature than most little girls do."

"I admit I don't like bugs and snakes," I said, "but I seemed different from my friends when I was at home. Many of the little girls in our neighborhood liked to stay indoors and play with their dolls. I did some of that, but I preferred being outside. I liked to climb trees, and I love animals. Dad says I'm a tomboy."

"You are different. That's what I like about you."

I didn't want to show it, but I felt a warm glow of satisfaction at Presley's compliment. He was proving to be the most amazing friend I had ever had.

Just before reaching the tunnel, I heard what sounded like soft meows followed by a hiss. Lowering my torch, I spotted a small recess in the wall. As I shone my light into the hole, I saw three pair of eyes staring back at me. "Look, Presley. Kittens! Aren't they adorable?" I said after picking one up.

Just then, hearing a low growl, I turned to see a gigantic cat glaring at me. Ears flattened, its green eyes were dilated. The hair was standing straight up on its back and head, and I could hear its long tail swishing angrily back and forth. This was no ordinary cat. Its body was sturdy and low to the ground, but even more frightening was the fact that it had huge, striated razor-sharp long fangs on each side of its mouth. I dropped the kitten immediately.

"Don't turn your back," Presley warned, grabbing my hand as we backed slowly toward the entrance of the tunnel. For each step we took backwards, the cat took a step forward. "Dive into the tunnel on the count of three," Presley instructed. "One, two, three."

As instructed, I dove into the tunnel. Turning my head, I saw Presley dive in behind me just as the cat made a swipe with its claw. When I saw Presley wasn't moving, I realized it was because the cat had pinned his foot to the ground. Its claw was much larger than a panther's or tiger's in the world we had come from. The enraged cat was trying to drag Presley backwards out of the tunnel. I knew that if it got him out in the open, it would stab him in the neck, slicing into a main artery with one of its fangs.

"Hang on," I yelled. I still had the stick that had served as a torch. Looking down, I saw that the end was still smoking. I maneuvered my body until I was next to Presley and edged past his leg. With a rush of adrenaline, I raised up and lunged forward, shoving the pointed end of the smoking torch deep into the cat's paw. A feline primal scream bounced off the cave walls before the cat released Presley's foot and beat a hasty retreat. "Move, Presley! Hurry before she comes back," I yelled.

After what seemed like forever, we managed to scramble out of the tunnel into the wide mouth of the cave. "Are you OK?" I asked frantically.

Even as I said the words, I realized Presley was not OK. His face was white, and blood was pouring out of his foot, spilling onto the ground. I grabbed the rope, coiled it, and after looping it around my neck, I put my arm around Presley's waist, holding him up as he began hopping, trying to avoid putting pressure on his injured foot. Once we got out of the cave, I tied one end of the rope around his waist. Then, I wrapped the other end of the rope three times around a large boulder. Holding onto my end, I planted my feet against the boulder for leverage. "Go ahead. I won't let you fall."

"I can't let you do this," Presley protested. "I can make it. Don't worry."

"I know, but just in case you slip, I've got you. Your foot looks like its mangled, you're bleeding, and we need to get back to the beach."

Holding my end of the rope, I braced myself as Presley made his way slowly down the rocks until he reached the ground. After he untied the rope, I pulled it up and again looped it around my neck. Then I carefully made my way down until I reached him. With Presley leaning on my shoulder, we headed back to the beach. It seemed to take forever, but we finally made it. Exhausted, Presley sat down on the ground and leaned back against a large rock. Crouching down, I looked at his foot. I tried to act like there was nothing out of the ordinary, but I was scared. The skin around the deep, ragged gash was swollen and blue. Gathering some dry moss and getting some clean water, I wiped the blood away, trying to be as gentle as possible. I then sat down next to Presley and pulled his head down onto my lap before saying a silent prayer. "Here I am again, God. I never know if you're there when I need you, but please help Presley. Don't let him get sick. Show me what to do."

After sitting quietly for a few minutes, I had an idea. I remembered watching a movie where a Native American medicine man put moss and leaves on a wounded man's injury. Without saying anything, I got up and started walking around. There were plenty of plants and moss, but which ones would work? I finally settled on a giant plant that resembled the aloe vera plants that grew in our garden at our home in Lakewood. Everyone knows that aloe vera plants have amazing healing properties. Breaking off some stalks and gathering more moss, I returned to Presley. Sitting down, I broke open the plant stem and carefully poured the juice on Presley's wound. I then covered it with moss and wrapped his foot in a palm frond. By this time, it was getting dark. We hadn't eaten, but neither of us was at all interested in food. Crawling into our shelter, we lay down. Our pets were unusually subdued. It was as if they could sense that Presley was hurt. I thought I wasn't tired, but I must have been because within minutes, I fell asleep.

I woke up the next morning to the usual morning noises of the surf moving gently over the sand, the buzz of insects, and the sound of birds. It took me a few minutes to remember the events of the previous evening. When I did, I sat up hurriedly. My heart sank when I saw Presley was gone. Scrambling out into the sunshine, I found him sitting by the rock that served as our table. "How is your foot?" I asked, trying not to let him see how worried I was.

"I'm fine," he smiled. "Look." He extended his leg. I was dumbfounded. The wound on his foot was completely healed. All that remained was a faint scar. It was only then that I allowed myself to cry.

Chapter 16

Presley and I agreed we would not return to the cave. That close encounter with the enraged saber-toothed cat was an experience we did not want to repeat.

"Do you think she'll come looking for us?" I asked Presley one morning.

"No, I think there's an exit out of the cavern that is far from where we are. Her priorities are her kittens. We are no longer a threat. She's probably forgotten all about us."

"I hope so. I don't want to run into her again."

"You're not alone," Presley said. glancing down at his foot. Even though it was completely healed, just the thought of that injury made both of us nervous.

By this time, we had established a routine that was so familiar we didn't even need to talk. In the mornings, we went to the jungle and picked nuts, fruit, and berries. My favorite fruit was a cross between a peach and a melon. When I bit into it, the juice was so delicious I sometimes groaned with pleasure. The berries, growing on bushes, were huge and vividly colored. Presley and I had taste-tested every fruit and berry we could find. Never once did we suffer any negative symptoms.

In the afternoons, we returned to the beach to fish and gather oysters. We swam, gathered seashells, and walked along the beach. One day, I realized we were no longer staring out at the horizon of the ocean hoping for rescue. "Have you given up?" I asked Presley.

"No, but hoping to see a boat and praying for rescue every day just makes me sad. Maybe one day I'll happen to look up, glance out, and spot a ship or a boat. For now, I've decided what will be, will be."

I didn't say anything, but I felt the same way.

We had both improved our culinary skills. One strange fruit we had discovered tasted like sweet potatoes. We would wrap them in leaves, let the fire burn down and bury them in the coals. After pulling them out and unwrapping them, the skins would be crisp. When we cut into them, the insides were crunchy. They were delicious. We did the same thing with the fish we caught after cleaning them.

By this time, we had become so accustomed to setting the rock table for meals we couldn't imagine doing anything else. As for Bingo and Bo Jangles, they acted like they were also developing table manners. While we ate, they sat side by side quietly waiting for us to finish. The minute we cleared the table, they made it clear it was time for them to eat.

Gizmo, on the other hand, was oblivious when it came to table manners, or manners of any kind for that matter. Every time we ate, he made a lot of irritated chirps to let us know he was bored as he waited for us to finish eating so he could play with his friends. "Why are you ignoring me?" he seemed to ask. He ate his fill each morning while we foraged in the jungle, stuffing himself with berries and nuts. We often laughed because after he ate, he crammed his mouth with berries and nuts until his cheeks bulged. He carried his leftovers around for hours.

"Do you think he's a little greedy?" I asked Presley one day after watching Gizmo's antics.

"Maybe he's saving for a rainy day," Presley laughed.

In many ways this was a magical kingdom. We were never ill, and any wound we suffered healed within hours. Not only could I see perfectly, but my hair was different. I noticed it one day when I caught my reflection while swimming in the small pool in the jungle. The image that stared back at me was not what I expected. Instead, it was a girl that could almost be described as attractive. Instead of the mat of white, tight curls I was accustomed to, my hair had grown, and the curls were looser. As I continued to stare, I noticed freckles scattered across my nose and cheekbones. They complimented my face. My eyes were a luminous emerald green. For the first time in my life, after being in the sun for hours, I had not experienced a bad sunburn. Instead, I had the beginning of a golden tan. "Is this really me?" I marveled. "Someday I might actually be pretty."

As for Presley, he was no longer thin. Instead of the stiff rigid walk I had seen when I first met him, he walked with an easy gait, and his movements were relaxed. Gold highlights were scattered through his dark hair, and somehow, without me realizing it, the cowlick that he had never been able to control was gone. His skin had a healthy glow, and his eyes danced.

"How can this be happening?" I wondered.

It was easy to forget we were lost as we laughed, played, and teased each other every day. After all, we were in paradise, but when the sun went down and we crawled into our shelter, we grew quiet. No matter how wonderful this place was, we missed our families and the world we had come from.

"Do you like it here?" I asked Presley one night.

"Yes, it's such an amazing place. The colors are amazing. They are so much more vivid than at home. I'm doing things I didn't even know I could do, but I worry about my mom and grandparents. I still want to go home."

"I do, too."

That night as we fell asleep, we fully expected that when we woke up the next morning, it would be just like every other day. We had no way of knowing it would go horribly wrong - so wrong that our magic kingdom would become a living hell.

Chapter 17

Looking back now on that horrific morning, I remember waking up with a strange sense of uneasiness. "It's probably just my imagination," I told myself as I crawled out of our shelter and looked around. As usual, the sun appeared to be a blurry ball of yellow light shining through the morning haze. Birds were wheeling and calling each other in the sky. The surge of the waves hitting the sand sounded the same as it always did. That familiar emptiness in my heart was familiar, too. I knew it wouldn't go away until I was able to get back to my father.

We made our trek to the jungle and gathered nuts and fruit. Gizmo, as usual, acted like he was starving as he gobbled his food, then stored more in his cheeks. As usual, we laughed.

Before long, we headed back to the beach. Presley got there first. When I caught up to him, he was crouched down, staring at something in the sand.

"What are you looking at?" I asked.

"Tracks. Some kind of animal has been here. It almost looks like a bird, but it's got four feet. Whatever it is, it's huge."

Peering down, I looked at the strange marks. Each track was at least three feet long. Curious, we both followed the tracks for a short distance until they seemed to end at a large circular mound.

"There's something under here," Presley said.

We each grabbed a stick and started to dig. About twelve inches down, we found a nest of eggs. Smaller in size than a hen would lay, these eggs had another unique difference. Instead of the typical shell, they were covered in what appeared to be soft leather. After carefully lifting them out, we put all twenty of them in a neat row.

I was still digging to make sure I hadn't missed anything when I happened to look up. "Did that egg just tremble?" I wondered. "It has to be my imagination," I decided as I resumed digging.

But it wasn't my imagination. I looked up again, and this time there were tiny movements. Then, the egg began rocking back and forth violently.

"Look Presley! It's going to hatch!" I said, my voice shaking with excitement. Within minutes, cracks began appearing in more of the eggs. When the first hatchling broke through, leaving a collapsed shell behind, it struggled to its feet.

"What the heck is it?" Presley asked. "I know turtles lay eggs in the sand, but this doesn't look like any turtle I've ever seen."

This strange little animal did not look like a baby chick either. Instead of feathers, it had gray scales, a short tail, long neck, leathery wings, and four feet. There was something familiar about it. Suddenly, I remembered a drawing I had seen in a book.

"Presley, guess what! It's a reptile," I said. "It's a Pterosaurs."

Opening its jaws, the hatchling made a noise that sounded like a piece of chalk scraping a blackboard. Presley and I covered our ears. Wobbling a little bit to get its balance, the creature began running around our feet in circles. It wasn't long before all the critters had broken through their shells. What had seemed like a blank section of the beach minutes earlier was suddenly alive with motion.

There was nothing sweet and cuddly about these little creatures, but babies of almost any kind are endearing. I couldn't help but think they were cute even if the noise they were making was hurting our ears. Leaning over, I picked one up. Cocking its head, it looked up at me expectantly. "I think it believes I'm its mother," I said.

We were so spellbound by the miniature dinosaurs running around in the sand we didn't realize that what had earlier seemed like a bird flying high overhead in the distance had glided downward until it was almost directly above us. We only looked up when Bingo began barking furiously. Bo Jangles clawed his way up my back and dived into my backpack even though it was partially filled with fruit and nuts. As for Gizmo, he was trying to burrow his way into my hair.

Shocked, at first all we could do was stare at the creature circling above our heads. With a twenty-foot wingspan, long neck, hooklike beak, and a body covered with leathery scales, it was not only enormous, it was terrifying. I was still holding the baby Pterosaurs when the monster screamed. It was the same scream I had heard when I first found myself on the beach after falling from the tree. The scream was so grating and shrill it seemed to bounce off the hills and echo back in one spine-tingling wail. That scream had scared me then, and now, seeing the creature that made that sound, I was terrified.

"Run," Presley yelled. "It's the mother!"

"Not again," I thought. "When will I learn to leave well enough alone. It was this mother's eggs, and she's going to kill us."

I can't remember ever running that fast. Yet, like something out of a nightmare, it seemed that no matter how fast I ran, my feet were barely moving as the creature swooped down. Even though I dropped the baby, the monster, propelled by its huge feet, galloped along behind us. I felt its hot breath scald my neck as one iron claw closed around my waist. Within seconds, I was airborne. Then, I heard another scream. Looking over, I saw Presley dangling from the creature's other claw. Using every ounce of strength I possessed, I struggled to get free. It was useless. The flying dinosaur was too big, I was too small, and its grip was too tight. "We'll never get free," I sobbed. "It's probably going to eat us. Please, God, if this is a dream, I want to wake up."

Just when I had given up hope, there was a blinding flash. A bolt of lightning seemed to split the sky. Coming to a halt in midair, almost as if it had hit an invisible barrier, the creature let out another horrible scream. It then dropped us. In a free fall, Presley and I fell head over heels until, with a thud, we hit the side of a grassy hill. After rolling a short distance, we came to a stop. Exhausted and terrified, we just lay there trying to catch our breath and process what had happened. Finally, we staggered to our feet. Bingo came racing over the hill. He had run along the ground, never letting the monster out of his sight. He, too, seemed exhausted as he flopped down at our feet. The backpack on my back started to move, and I heard loud meows coming from it. I opened it, and Bo Jangles sprang out. He sat down next to Bingo and gave me a reproachful look. Gizmo had never let go of my hair. I could feel the nails on his feet and hands digging into my scalp. Carefully lifting him down, I sat him next to his canine and feline friends. I almost started to apologize.

"Are you OK?" Presley asked.

"I think so, but I'm pretty shaken up."

"Screech! Screech!" The terrible screams were directly over our heads. Standing in knee deep grass, we craned our necks as we watched what seemed to be a battle in the sky. The predator who dropped us seemed to be fighting, but where was its attacker? All we could see were jagged lines of light that seemed to be tearing the sky apart. For several minutes, we watched the creature as it was buffeted by what seemed to be an electric current that encased its body. When it fell, it landed not far from us with so much force, the ground shook.

What happened next still brings tears to my eyes.

"Sophie, Presley, run! Hurry! I'm over here." It was my mother's voice. I had come to believe I would never hear her voice again. I couldn't believe what I was hearing.

"Mom? Where are you?"

"I'm over here. Hurry. You don't have much time."

Spinning around, I saw her standing at the top of a hill, her slender silhouette framed against the sky. As beautiful as ever, she was dressed in white. Light not only seemed to be radiating in an arc around her, but it was radiating through her.

Grabbing each other's hands, Presley and I began to run, but even though we should have been getting closer, with each step we took, my mother seemed further away. When we reached the top of the hill, she was gone. "Am I reliving that awful recurring dream I used to have when I lived with Aunt Rose?" I wondered.

Looking around frantically, I spotted her again. This time, she was at the foot of another hill and was standing next to a tree. To my amazement, it was the same tree from the courtyard at the Stagecoach Inn.

"It's the tree!" Presley yelled. "How did it get here?"

We ran down the hill as fast as we could. When I reached her, I threw my arms around her. "I thought I'd never see you again," I sobbed. "I've missed you, and Dad misses you, too."

"I know, darling." She put her hands on each side of my face and looked into my eyes. Gazing at me with love and compassion, she kissed the top of my head, something she had done as early as I could remember.

"I'm sorry I said I hated you. I didn't mean it. I promise, I'll never say anything like that again."

"Of course, you didn't mean it. I knew that. You were upset. Sometimes we say things we don't mean when our anger gets the best of us. I've always known how much you love me. You have a big heart, Sophie. It's one of the things that makes you special."

I felt a huge sense of relief. I hadn't realized how much those awful words I had spoken in anger had haunted me. Finally, Mom stepped away from me and turned to Presley. Smiling, she took his hand. "You're a wonderful friend, Presley. Take care of my sweet girl."

When I looked at Presley, he was standing straight as an arrow, and his face was serious. "It will be my honor," he said with a slight bow. Even though he was just a kid, in many ways, he was a young adult who was wise beyond his years.

Somehow Gizmo had reappeared and was once again clinging to my hair. Carefully removing him, Mom said, "You started this whole thing, little one. You went where you don't belong. You're not going anywhere." To my surprise, after staring at Mom for a minute, Gizmo hung his head. I think he was embarrassed and maybe even a little bit ashamed.

Bingo and Bo Jangles stayed perfectly still when Mom leaned over and gently picked them up. After carefully putting them in my backpack and before I could protest, she led me to the tree and boosted me up onto a lower branch.

"You have to get out of here," she told us. "Presley, make sure Sophie goes with you. Don't let her stay. Climb and don't look back."

Without a minute's hesitation, Presley began scrambling up the tree.

"Mom, aren't you coming? You must. We need you. Dad has been sad, and only you can make him happy." I was crying again because I realized she wasn't coming. How could she do this? I felt like my heart was breaking.

"I'm sorry, darling. I can't. Just remember, even though you can't see me, I'm with you. I'm in your mind and in your heart."

"No!" I screamed. "Why are you saying that? It's not enough. If you're not coming, I'm not going."

Presley, who had pulled himself up to a higher branch, reached down, yanked my shirt, and pulled. Screaming and crying, I fought. Even though I was taller than Presley, he was stronger. In fact, since we had fallen into this strange world, he was stronger than ever. As I felt myself being drawn upward, I glanced down just in time to see my mother's image blur then fade.

"I hate you, Presley," I wailed. "Let go of me! I want my mother." Immediately after telling Presley I hated him, I grew quiet. I didn't hate Presley. He was my best friend.

"No!" he yelled. "You heard her. We aren't supposed to be here. We have to get back."

Part of me wanted to stay with my mother, but the other part of me wanted to return to my father. No matter what, I had to give one of them up. Tearfully, I looked down one last time. I believe if I had seen my mother again, I never would have been able to leave. She was gone. My heart ached, but I knew if I went back, I would never find her. She had saved our lives. Thinking back to the overwhelming love in her eyes when she smiled at me, I realized she had never been mad. I had carried all that guilt for nothing. It was that thought that gave me the courage to do as she asked, even if it meant leaving her in this strange land. Using my feet for traction, I began to climb, slowly making my way up higher into the tree.

Chapter 18

Climbing to the top of the tree seemed to take days, but then time sped up. Darkness came, then light, then darkness again. With each new dawn, Presley and I would find ourselves staring at a landscape that was totally different from the day before. At first, daytime seemed to last a few hours before night fell, but then time sped up again. Now, it seemed there were just minutes between dawn and dusk. Days and nights began flashing by with lightning speed. Like spectators watching one preview after another in a movie theater, we saw the ocean pull back and the shoreline recede until it was no longer visible.

Exhausted, I closed my eyes. I must have dozed off for a minute because when I opened them, time had ground to a halt. The world around us had changed once again. I stared out at this new, but familiar, landscape in wonder. Very similar to the world we had come from, everything was lush and green. Gigantic dragonflies and huge butterflies filled the air. I could hear the birds singing. Suddenly, they grew quiet. An unearthly feline scream filled the air. "I wonder if it's a saber-toothed tiger who just found a meal?" I asked myself, thinking back to our close call with the angry cat that had tried to pull Presley out of the tunnel.

Then I heard a rumble. When the tree shook, I realized the ground was shaking. In disbelief, Presley and I stared as the ground tore apart in large rifts. In the distance, there was an enormous flare of orange and red flames along with debris that rose in the shape of a black pillar that seemed to be shooting out of a mountain top.

"It's a volcano!" I yelled.

"I know!" Presley yelled back.

We watched in horror as a huge cloud of ash headed our way, and the red magma flowed down the mountain, encasing everything in its path. I was relieved when I thought it was snowing until I realized those huge flakes coming down were not snow. They were ash that gradually blanketed a landscape that no longer seemed alive. The sun, which had been shining earlier, was obliterated. Choking because of the dust, we were both finding it hard to breathe.

"Do you think the magma will reach us?" I yelled.

"No. I think we're safe as long as we stay in this tree."

Minutes later, it seemed like the entire earth shook as a giant rock came hurtling through the air. It split the land, leaving a gaping hole. "It's a meteor!" Presley yelled. "Nothing can survive all of this."

I was sad as I thought about Gizmo and all the living things we had enjoyed in our magical kingdom.

The world changed once again. The volcano, the fire, the magma flow, and the ash were gone. The tropical vista had been transformed into a winter wonderland. With our ringside seats, Presley and I, still sitting on the limb of the tree, found ourselves staring out on a large snowdrift.

This was not the snowfall I had experienced growing up in Dallas. I thought about those winter storms that were few and far between. When they did come, the schools closed. Accidents and out-of-control cars sliding on black ice dominated the news. Grocery store shelves emptied rapidly while people stocked up. Mom used to laugh at that. "You'd think we were going to be snowed in for six months," she would say. Many of us were excited, and the mood was jubilant, but those storms only lasted a few days.

In the place we were now, this storm was something entirely different. Snow was piling up fast, and it was already deep, deeper than anything I had ever seen. From all appearances, it had been snowing for some time. Reaching out, I caught a snowflake in the palm of my hand. I was fascinated by its complex design. "Presley, did you know that no two snowflakes are alike?"

"Right now, I couldn't care less. I'm freezing."

I realized I was freezing, too. In fact, I don't think I had ever been that cold in my life.

"Presley, what's happening? It's snowing so hard I can't see anything."

I could barely get the words out through my chattering teeth. The snow was even piling up on our heads and arms. Peering out between branches that had been green and leafy just minutes earlier but were now stark and bare, I spotted huge forms. Moving slowly out of what appeared to be a blizzard, they were heading toward the tree. As they lumbered forward, the ground began to shake. Clutching the trunk of the tree, Presley and I hung on for dear life, trying not to fall. Although they resembled elephants, they were bigger than any elephant I have ever seen. Their shaggy coats almost reached the ground, and their long ivory tusks arched outward in graceful curves. The massive animal who seemed to be leading the herd with its trunk moving slowly back and forth seemed to be searching the landscape for hidden dangers. By its side walked a baby. With its small trunk moving in the air and ears flapping in the wind, the baby looked like something out of a Walt Disney movie. As the procession moved past, not one of those beasts looked our way.

"They're mammoths," Presley whispered.

"I know. Aren't they wonderful?" Not hearing a response, I looked over at Presley and was shocked to see icicles hanging from his eye lashes. Frost had crystallized into a crust that covered his hair.

I was finding it harder and harder to breathe. With each breath I took, icy air stabbed my lungs, tears stung my eyes, and my whole body was shivering uncontrollably. Minutes later, I knew it was a bad sign when the shivering stopped as the cold penetrated deep into my bones.

"We're freezing to death," I wailed. "I hate the cold."

A few minutes later, I could no longer feel the cold. Instead, I felt strangely warm and sleepy. I was tired, and my eyelids were so heavy I could barely keep them open.

"Presley, I'm going to take a nap."

"Don't do it!" he shouted as he leaned over and shook me. "You can't go to sleep. It's hypothermia. You'll never wake up."

"Too sleepy," I mumbled. "Sorry, Presley."

Sometime later I did wake up, and when I did, Presley was awake, too. "Presley! We're still alive!"

"Yes," Presley said with a relieved look on his face. "Fortunately, that ice age didn't last long enough to kill us."

Everything around us was green again, but the forest was vanishing. Even as we watched, the trees became indistinct, shrinking into the ground until there were only a few remaining. What appeared next was a prairie. Seemingly out of nowhere, Native Americans appeared as if out of a dream. Moving silently in single file along a creek, they were slender and muscular. Their coppery skin glowed with perspiration. Many of them wore nothing but breach cloths. Boys, walking behind the adults, wore little adornment. Those who were older had feathers and beads woven into their braids. The most frightening thing was their faces. At first, I thought they were wearing masks, but with a shock, I realized it was war paint. It was meant to frighten, and it did. Many of them were carrying bows held down at their sides with arrows already notched. When they finally disappeared, I breathed a sigh of relief.

Again, our surroundings seemed to blur and fade. We found ourselves staring minutes later at a cloud of dust moving rapidly along what was now a dirt road. Appearing out of this dirty mirage, a stagecoach pulled by six black horses raced by. Sitting in the driver's position on top, a slight figure dressed in black handled the whip skillfully. The whip never actually touched the horses, but instead, it cracked over their heads. I got the feeling that for the horses, this was a marvelous game to see how fast they could run.

We watched as the stagecoach pulled up in front of a two-story white building, complete with wooden pillars and a wide veranda that seemed to have magically appeared in what had once been an empty field. When the coach came to a stop, two small boys jumped off the porch, ran forward, and opened the stagecoach doors.

The first one to step out of the stagecoach was a stern looking man. I got a glimpse of the star-shaped badge on his vest when he turned back, leaned over, and held out his hand. A slender gloved hand, clad in lace, reached out and placed fingers in the palm of his large hand. Out stepped a beautiful woman, immaculately groomed. Her dress was black and white plaid silk. A straw hat with a jaunty feather was perched atop her carefully arranged blonde hair. Holding the edge of her skirt gingerly as her feet touched the ground, she looked back.

"Come on, children, we're at the hotel," she said.

The next one to emerge was a little girl. Approximately six years old, she was dressed in a white cotton dress with puffed sleeves. A blue satin ribbon was tied at the waist. With a sturdy build and determined jaw, it was evident she had a strong personality, but the most outstanding feature about her was her hair. The color of ripe golden wheat, it hung in soft waves that cascaded down her back. "I would kill for hair like that," I thought wistfully.

The next one out of the carriage was a dark-haired boy. With a slight grin, he glanced around to make sure no one was watching. Then, reaching forward, he grabbed a handful of the little girl's hair and yanked.

"Stop it, Tom," she yelled. "Aunt Elizabeth, Tom pulled my hair."

"Children, behave," the woman responded, her manner distracted as she watched the luggage being stacked on the ground. "Tom, quit pestering your sister."

"You're nothing but a big baby, Isadora," I heard Tom whisper into his sister's ear.

"I'll get you later. Just you wait."

The last one out was a young girl who wore a gingham dress. Slim and graceful, she appeared to be in her teens. Her long, chestnut hair hung in a braid down the middle of her back. Taking each child by the hand, she said, "Tom, if you don't stop teasing your sister, and Isadora if you don't quit being so dramatic, I won't tell you a story tonight."

"Sorry, Hayley," Tom replied, hanging his head.

As for Isadora, she looked at Hayley with adoration. "Hayley, you are the best cousin in the world. We love your stories. I promise, we'll be good."

Hayley laughed. "We'll see for how long."

Presley and I watched them in amazement as they entered the hotel.

Next, the driver climbed down. Small in stature, he was slim. I wondered how someone that small could handle a team of six large horses and do so with so much skill. Even more surprising was the fact he was wearing a long leather coat and gloves – strange apparel for this Texas heat. A man standing in the doorway of the hotel came down the steps to greet him. For a few minutes, they engaged in conversation. Then, the young girl in gingham came rushing out the door. Practically dancing down the steps, she rushed over to the driver.

"I just want you to know a lot of people are talking about you," she said. "Everyone says you're brave and an excellent driver. Some people say they only travel when they know you're driving. They know you won't take risks, and they also know you're a brave man who's a crack shot. Robberies on the road have almost stopped since you've taken over."

"Well, thank you, Ma'am. I much appreciate it," the driver said, touching his forefinger to the brim of his hat. Before she could say anything else, he turned and hurried away, heading to the stables in the back.

"Did I say anything wrong?" Hayley asked the tall blonde man who had been talking to the driver.

"No, Ma'am. Charlie is just shy."

"It's the Stagecoach Inn," Presley whispered. "I wonder what year this is."

I couldn't answer. I was too tired to be surprised. So much had happened so fast it was more than my mind could process. Earlier, I had been so sad my heart had ached. Now, I just felt numb. As I watched, the day was again transformed by a glorious Texas sunset followed by nightfall. Sadly, I gazed up at the stars sparkling against the black, velvet sky. Trapped in this strange world where time kept moving faster and faster, all I could think about was that I had again lost my mother. "Will I ever see her again?" I wondered. Then, deliberately pushing that thought from my mind, I decided the only way to ease the pain was to think about my father. "No matter what, I have one parent left," I decided. "It's time to get back to him."

"I have to get back to my father, Presley," I said.

"Don't leave without me," he pleaded. I didn't answer him. Instead, I loosened my grasp on the branch I had been clinging to, closed my eyes, and let myself fall. Everything went black.

Chapter 19

"Sophie, Sophie! Wake up!"

At first, Dad's voice sounded very far away. I kept my eyes squeezed shut because I didn't want to wake up. I was afraid if I opened my eyes, I would be confronted by a dinosaur, fang-toothed tiger, volcano, blizzard, or all of them. But Dad was persistent. I realized after a few minutes I wasn't going to be able to go back to sleep, and the sense of foreboding was beginning to fade, just as it does when you wake from a nightmare and realize it's not real. Finally, I opened my eyes. With his face inches from mine, Dad's eyes were wide with concern.

"Thank heavens you're awake. You've been asleep for hours."

"Where am I?"

"You're in our room at the Stagecoach Inn."

"How did I get here," I asked.

The look on Dad's face had changed from one of alarm to one of reproach. "About 3 a.m., I heard Bingo outside barking and scratching at the door. I didn't even know you were gone until I turned on the light. I rushed outside and ran into Charlotte. She was headed for our room because Presley was missing, too. We were afraid you had both been kidnapped. Presley's mom, the entire staff, and I were outside with flashlights looking for you. We feared the worst and were ready to call the police when we found both of you sleeping under the tree. Why on earth would you go out in the middle of the night? What were you thinking?"

"We saw something in the tree and wanted to check it out," I said sheepishly.

"When we woke you up, you were both incoherent, talking about volcanoes, seashells, mammoths, and a cave. We could only assume both of you fell and hit your heads after climbing the tree. We were going to take you to the hospital, but once you woke up, you both insisted you were fine. Presley went with his mother, and you came here, fell into bed, and immediately went to sleep. You've been asleep for hours."

I was silent for a moment. My last memory was letting myself fall out of the tree. I had no memory of being asleep on the lawn or of being awakened by a group of concerned adults. In fact, I had no memory of coming back to our room and going back to sleep.

"What time is it?"

"It's two in the afternoon. I was afraid if I let you sleep any longer, you wouldn't be able to sleep tonight. Sophie, you are, and have always been, a great kid. So is Presley, and I know you're both smart enough to know there are consequences for your actions. Charlotte and I are going to meet this afternoon to talk about this. She's unhappy that you went outside in the middle of the night, and frankly, so am I. That was dangerous. Anything could have happened."

With a jolt, memories began flooding my mind. As if watching a Technicolor movie, I saw what seemed like an endless sea, a waterfall, a beautiful pond complete with floating water lilies, and strange plants. I also saw enormous butterflies and dragonflies. "Everything is bigger in Texas," I thought, "but not that big."

Then, in my mind, I saw Presley running down a beach. The image was not life sized but small. It was like looking in the wrong end of a telescope. The word Gizmo popped into my mind, followed by the image of a tiny animal with an endearing face. The images then took on a nightmarish quality as I saw Presley and me being chased. We were airborne, struggling in the claws of a huge, flying monster. Not only did I see the images, but I also felt remnants of the emotions I had experienced that included dread and hopelessness, followed by the fatalistic decision that we were about to suffer a horrible death. Then, I remembered how Mom saved our lives.

Sitting up suddenly, I threw my arms around Dad's neck and nearly knocked him off the bed. With my head on his shoulder, I breathed in his fresh, clean smell, one that reminded me of prairies and ocean breezes.

"Dad, I saw Mom. She saved us! She's alive! She's more beautiful than ever! She even glows. She has an aura. It's amazing! She helped Presley and me get back to the tree. I think she fought the Pterosaurs. It would have killed us. She was wonderful."

Even before the words were out of my mouth, I felt Dad's body stiffen. He stayed motionless for what seemed like forever, as if he were shielding himself from pain. Moving back a little, I stared into his face. Seeing the pain and disbelief in his eyes, my heart sank.

"So, if you saw your mother, where is she?" he asked carefully.

"We were in a strange place. I think, for the most part, we were in prehistoric Texas. I believe Mom is trapped there. We need to go get her."

"I think you had a dream," Dad said hesitantly. "You've been through a lot, and I know you miss your mother. I do, too. You've always been creative and imaginative. Sometimes, when we miss someone so much, our minds can fool us into thinking we see them. I still have moments when I think I see your mother walking down the street, but it is someone who has hair like hers or someone who has the same body language."

As I looked at Dad, I felt ashamed knowing that I had caused him pain. I fought to control tears. The images, so vivid in my mind just moments ago, were beginning to fade and blur. Hearing his words, I begin to have doubts. Did any of this really happen, or was it like Dad said - just a dream? The Stagecoach Inn is miles away from the ocean, but I remembered that when I came to after falling out of the tree, I was on a beach staring out at a vast expanse of water.

Dad took my hand. "Don't worry, Sophie," he said. "We'll put this behind us. However, I do have some news. It could be a clue about your mother's disappearance. Mike called this morning. A Vietnamese gardener showed up in his office. He found one of your mom's earrings. He doesn't speak very good English, so it was difficult to understand him. Mike said the man seemed frightened. Did your mom know anyone from Vietnam?"

"She did a story once about a community garden that sold fruit and vegetables to the public. Mom always bought our produce there. I think the gardeners were from Vietnam. They seemed to like her a lot."

"Why don't you take a shower and get dressed. I need to run an errand. When I get back, we'll go to the dining room to meet with Charlotte and Presley. By the way, where are your glasses?"

It took me a minute to process the question as another image flashed in my mind. I saw my glasses lying on a large rock, smashed beyond repair. "If I've imagined all of this," I wondered, "how did I break my glasses? And are they really broken?" But deep down I knew my glasses were broken. What was strange was that as I looked around the room, I could see better than I've ever been able to see in my entire life.

"I broke them," I replied. "They're ruined."

"That's OK. You're due for a visit to the optometrist anyway. Your eye exam is overdue, so I'll make an appointment. Will you be alright until then?"

"Dad, don't worry. I don't need them anymore. I can see perfectly." Dad just stood there looking at me skeptically. As he kept staring at me, I grew uncomfortable.

A few minutes later as I stood under the hot shower, my mind was spinning. If I imagined this whole thing, where were my glasses? Were they really broken? If nothing had changed, my vision should be giving me fits. Everything should be blurry. Instead, I was seeing colors, objects, and people perfectly. I remembered looking at Dad's face. It was almost as if I was seeing him for the first time. Even when I wore glasses, I had never seen his features in such detail. Now, every line, the crinkles around his eyes, and the humorous tilt to his mouth were amazingly clear.

My mind then moved on to what Dad had said about the gardener who found Mom's earring. According to Dad, there was no doubt that the earring was Mom's. They had her initials engraved on the back.

I then thought of another mystery we had experienced. When Presley and I found ourselves in that strange world, it seemed like we were there for months. We really had been gone for only four hours, but even now, the memories were continuing to blur, just like a dream that is so vivid when you are experiencing it but fades into nothingness when you wake up. I didn't want this to happen. I had seen my mother. She was alive! I needed proof, and somehow that proof was connected to the tree. I also realized it would be hard to prove. "I wonder if anyone else saw Gizmo," I wondered. "If we can find him, maybe people will believe us."

After I stepped out of the tub, I wrapped myself in a large towel, went into the living room, and pulled back the drapes. I looked outside and stared at the perfectly manicured yard and the ancient tree. In daylight, it seemed harmless. The road leading to the highway and the small town of Salado could have been a scene typical of many small towns across Texas. It looked the same as it did the day Dad and I arrived. I thought about the strange occurrences of time. When Mom put us in the tree, time as we know it seemed to stand still. Then, it sped up until it seemed to be spinning so fast Presley and I could hardly comprehend what we were seeing. And what about the ice age? I have always lived in a climate that, for the most part, was warm. I would never forget that biting cold. We had not only seen it, we had felt it. It didn't seem possible, but somehow, I believed Presley and I had experienced the impossible. Nothing made sense.

After pacing around the room, I went back into the bathroom and forced myself to look in the mirror over the sink. Because I was back in *real* time in the *real* world, I expected to see the scrawny kid with the crazy hair who knew she was destined to grow up ugly. Instead, I barely recognized the face that gazed back at me. Something had happened in my magical world when it came to my appearance, and somehow, I had brought it back to the present time. "Wow," I thought. "I'm almost pretty." My face was filled out, and for the first time in my life, I was slightly tanned without a sign of sunburn. My cheeks were pink, and instead of my hair being frizzy, it seemed a little longer and framed my face in loose curls. Those curls were the color of platinum shaded with strands of gold. Even my mouth looked different. My lips were fuller and a deeper shade of pink. Just like the day I had caught my reflection in the pond by the waterfall, my eyes were an intense shade of green

Moving back to the bedroom, I pulled a clean shirt out of a drawer. Spotting my old pair of jeans draped over a chair, I put them on, barely aware of my movements. I was still trying to sort out images that were crowding my brain. "I've got to stop thinking about this," I told myself. "I'm getting a headache. Maybe I did hit my head. On the other hand, I could be losing my mind."

I couldn't wait to see Presley and tell him about this so-called dream. If he didn't know what I was talking about, I would have to accept the fact that I had either been dreaming, or I'd experienced a series of hallucinations. On the other hand, if Presley said he had had the same experience, it had to be real.

When Dad walked in, I felt a wave of apprehension. "Dad, are you mad at me?" I asked when he sat down across from me at the small table.

"No, Sophie. I want to talk to you about your mom."

"OK."

"Tell me more about the garden co-op run by the Vietnamese people."

'You mean the one she wrote the story about?"

"Yes. Where is it located?"

"It's on Fitzhugh Avenue in Dallas, not too far from our old house in Lakewood."

"Did she go there a lot?"

"Yes. She really admired those people. She thought they were not only hard working, but she also felt like they were very smart. Why?"

"I just called Mike, and he said he's talked further with the man that found your mom's earring. Mike said the man claimed he found the earring at the back of the garden when he was raking. He also said strange things were happening in the garden. He claimed things were growing three times faster and bigger than they were in the rest of the garden, and many of their children, who were often with them when they weren't in school, talked about the white lady who often appeared, seemingly out of nowhere. They said she was very beautiful, but she also seemed very sad."

"How did the man know the earring was Mom's?" I asked.

"Mike said he asked the man that same question. Because she visited often and because she was beautiful and friendly, the man said they noticed the earrings she wore every time she stopped by. He told Mike he and everyone who worked there were sad when they read about your mom's disappearance in the newspaper."

For a few minutes, Dad and I were quiet as we tried to make sense of this new information.

"Do you think she lost an earring during one of her visits?" Dad asked.

"No, Dad. Mom loved those earrings. She wore them all the time. I used to tease her because a lot of times she wore them to bed. When she did take them off, she left them on the dresser. If she had lost one, she would have told me. In fact, I remember she was wearing them the night she disappeared."

My mind went back to the story Mom wrote about the co-op. I remember her saying how angry Bill Crankshaw was when she wrote the story and insisted on running it. He told her it was a waste of her time and a waste of space in the magazine.

"Why bother with these immigrants," Mom told me he had said. "They don't have a dime. They're nothing. No one cares about them."

"Mom said Bill wanted the focus of the magazine to be on wealthy, high-society people. She said she hadn't realized what a snob he was and that she made a huge mistake bringing him into the business."

Dad's face was grim. "Yes, it was a mistake."

Baffled, Dad and I just sat and stared at each other for a few minutes. Finally, we got up and headed out the door.

Thinking about everything I had experienced in the last twenty-four hours (or thought I had experienced) along with this new information about Mom that was equally unsettling, I wondered if I would ever learn what was real and what was not.

There was one person who had always been able to help me sort things out any time I got confused. It was Mom. "I'd give anything to have you back Mom," I told her in my mind. "I don't think Dad or I will ever let you out of our sight again."

Chapter 20

Because I knew Charlotte was upset with both Presley and me, I wasn't surprised to see her sitting next to Presley when Dad and I walked into the dining room. The look on her face was stern. As for Presley, he was staring fixedly at his plate. I knew I was in for a lecture.

"Sophie, I am so disappointed in both of you. What were you thinking?"

"Mom, come on," Presley interjected. Then, to my amazement, he told a lie. "It was all my idea. We just climbed a tree in the courtyard. We didn't even leave the grounds."

I sat there silently, not knowing what to say. Presley reached for my hand under the tablecloth and squeezed it. Even though I stared straight ahead, I felt a slow blush cover my cheeks.

"That's not the point," Charlotte said. "It was the middle of the night. Not only could you have fallen and hurt yourself badly, but you could have ruined your hands." After saying that, she happened to glance over at Presley's hands and turned pale. It was as if she had noticed them for the first time. "Speaking of your hands, what in the world have you been doing? Your hands look awful. I hope this won't affect your ability to play the piano."

I felt Presley's irritation even though we hadn't spoken to each other.

"My hands are fine, Mom. I can't live in a glass bubble just so I can grow up to be a concert pianist."

"That's enough, Presley." Turning to me, Charlotte said, "Sophie, we were worried sick. To make matters worse, Presley has been telling me the wildest stories. I can't imagine how he's come up with all of this. Telling wild tales is fine for entertainment, but this is no laughing matter. I want you to tell me the truth."

I felt my mood lighten even though we were both in trouble. Presley must have had the same experiences I did. Just like Dad, Charlotte thought we had made it all up. "Maybe I hadn't been dreaming after all," I thought.

"But it is true," I protested. "We tried to catch a little animal that we thought was a monkey, but it was a Crusafontia. There used to be a lot of them, not only in Texas, but all over the Southwest. They're extinct now. That's why we climbed the tree. We ended up falling out of the tree, but then we found ourselves by an ocean. We got caught by a huge Pterosaurs. Mom saved us. We were afraid we'd never get home."

Speechless, Charlotte just stared at me, not knowing how to respond. Seeing the stunned looks on both Dad's and Charlotte's faces, I stopped. It was obvious they didn't believe us, and who could blame them? The story sounded crazy, even to me.

"It's obvious that both of you are very creative," Dad interjected. "I think you've been watching too many computer games. You need to be careful that you don't lose touch with reality."

"Mom, you've always told me you didn't want me to spend so much time on the computer," Presley interjected. "Since Sophie got here, I haven't wanted to play computer games once. I didn't have anything to do before she came here."

"I know you are friends," Charlotte said, "and I appreciate that. I think it's wonderful that you are spending so much time outdoors, even though it's taking a toll on your hands, but you both need to be more considerate. Sophie, I've talked to your father, and we both agree there needs to be consequences. You are both grounded."

"What!!!" Presley said. "Do you expect us to sit around all day in our rooms?"

"No, Chris and I have something else in mind. You are not to go outside unless it's to help people with their luggage. You can swim in the late afternoon for thirty minutes when your chores are done. Sophie, you will help in the kitchen. Presley, you will pick up all the trays out-side the rooms and take them to the kitchen. Also, we are taking your cell phones. Any chores that need to be done, I expect them to get done without you complaining. As far as I'm concerned, you're both getting off lightly. Chris and I are going to a meeting. I expect you to be on your best behavior."

"How long will we be grounded?" Presley asked.

"It depends on how you conduct yourselves in the coming days. We'll let you know," Charlotte replied before she and Dad walked out of the dining room.

For a few minutes, Presley and I were silent.

"I'm glad you told your mom we were by an ocean and that there were dinosaurs," I said, pushing my food around on my plate.

"You told your dad, too. I wanted Mom to understand, but I guess she just can't wrap her mind around it."

"Neither can I. When I told my dad I saw Mom and that she is alive, he didn't believe me. In fact, he didn't believe anything I told him. I wish I hadn't said anything. All I've done is make him sadder than he already is."

"Me, too," Presley said. "Mom has always stressed how important it is to be truthful. I feel bad that I've upset her. Now I'm afraid she won't believe anything I say in the future."

"Presley, do you think we were dreaming? If so, how could we both have the same dream?"

"I don't know. Even though it seemed so real at the time, when I think about it, it's too freaking crazy."

Mystified, we both grew quiet. Once my favorite food, the ham-burger and French fries seemed totally unappetizing. I could see grease glistening on the fries, and the meat in the hamburger looked repulsive. Listlessly, I pushed the food around on my plate as I thought longingly of the roasted oysters, crab meat, luscious fruits, and berries my brain was insisting we had eaten just hours earlier. It seemed we both had en-joyed a diet that was free of chemicals. We had eaten food that was not processed. Food that was not only delicious, but moments after eating it, we could almost feel the nourishment energizing our bodies. "If none of this was true, how would I know the difference between that food and this," I wondered. Glancing over at Presley, I realized he was pushing his food around, too.

"It is totally unappetizing, isn't it?" I asked.

"Yes. How can this be? How can we both have had the same dreams, ones that seemed to take days and even months, yet the events happened in the space of four hours?"

"I don't know, but something had to have happened. By the way, have you looked in the mirror? Your cowlick seems to be gone. It looks like you've put on some weight. You've got muscles."

"That's a good thing," Presley replied with a grin. "You're looking great. Do you still see well without your glasses?"

"Yes. I told Dad, but I don't think he believes me. He's taking me to the optometrist next week."

"Hmm. That should be interesting," Presley commented. "I wonder how the doctor will explain that?"

I sneezed. It suddenly occurred to me that the real world seemed almost as dangerous as the world we had come from. In that prehistoric land, the air was pure and clean. Here, even with air conditioning, I could almost feel the particles of pollution floating in the air surrounding us. I sneezed again. Hoping to find a tissue, I reached into my jean pocket. Instead of a tissue, my fingers closed around a hard object. Pulling it out, I opened my hand. A large, luminous gray pearl was nestled in the center of my palm. Staring at its shimmering surface, I turned it slightly. For a moment, I thought I caught an image of Mom's face, but then it vanished. "It was Mom!" I said, my voice trembling with emotion. "She is alive."

"Wow, that is so cool," Presley exclaimed as he stared down at the pearl. "We weren't dreaming, and this pearl proves it."

"We've got to go back. I know Mom's there. We have to find her."

"We will," Presley said. "We just have to figure out when and how."

Chapter 21

When I got back to my room, I saw my cell phone on the nightstand. Dad may have forgotten to take it, but I suspect he didn't want me to be without it. He had always stressed he wanted me to be able to get in touch with him. He hadn't said anything when Charlotte said she was taking our cell phones. My intuition told me he didn't agree.

I picked up the phone and called Amy. She was silent as I told her about Presley's and my adventure. Occasionally, she would interject a question. "Presley had the same experience as I did," I said. "No one believes us. My dad and Charlotte had almost convinced us we'd imagined the whole thing. It was a magical place, but it was also dangerous. We almost died a couple of times. The strange thing is that when Presley's foot got mangled by a saber-toothed tiger, I thought he'd either die from an infection or end up crippled. His foot healed overnight."

"Have you any proof that what you experienced was real?" Amy asked.

"Yes. When we first got there, we began harvesting oysters. When I opened the shells, many of them contained large, beautiful pearls. I stuck one in my pants pocket, forgot about it, and accidentally brought it back. Also, I broke my glasses when I fell out of the tree, but now my vision is perfect. I see everything clearly. In fact, I suspect, my vision is not only perfect but is beyond perfect. Somehow, we went back in time. Do you believe me?"

"Yes," Amy answered after a long silence. I'm going to talk to my mother. I'll call you back." Fifteen minutes later my cell phone rang. It was Amy. "My mom knows you're telling the truth. She said to watch out for that tree. Some of the Dinka tribe in Africa are afraid of certain trees. A lot of people think it's because they're afraid of the snakes that hide in the branches, but that's not the only reason. They know that certain trees are haunted. You need to stay away from it."

"I can't, Amy. I have to go back and find my mother."

"Maybe there's another way."

"There could be, but I don't think so."

"I'm going to talk to our elders," Amy said. "Maybe I can find someone who can give you advice." Amy called me a couple of days later. "I talked to the elders," she said. "They said that you have to go back to the tree. Even if you don't find your mother, you will find answers."

When I hung up, I was more confused than ever.

During the next couple of weeks, Presley and I were on our best behavior. Presley pushed a cart as he gathered trays littered with dirty dishes, cups, leftover food, and garbage into the kitchen. There was stuff on those trays I hated to even touch. It's amazing the things people put on trays when they leave them outside their doors in hotels. No matter how disgusting the trays were, Presley didn't say a word as he gathered them up, and I didn't complain once as I emptied them and scraped off the plates. Working in the kitchen, my job was to load the dishwasher. At first, the cooks were irritable when I showed up. I think they thought I would just be in the way. They knew my dad and I were friends with the owner, and they thought I would expect special treatment. When they saw how hard I worked without complaining, I won them over. They started giving me special treats. Before long, the chef was telling me about his close calls with culinary failures, and he even began sharing tips he used in preparing certain dishes. The guy truly loved to cook. Even though a lot of the recipes on the menus had been used for years, he lived for finding old, out-of-print cookbooks as he searched for that forgotten recipe that would win him a place on a national cooking show. Daily he would ask me to taste one of his latest concoctions. "Stop," I said one day as I laughed. "If I keep this up, I'm going to get fat." Pedro, the porter, even started teaching me Spanish. I managed to control my temper one day when a large red-headed kid threw me in the deep end of the pool. When I came up for air, he was standing at the edge of the pool grinning like an ape. "If he just knew how much I'd like to kick him in the butt," I fumed. Instead, I just smiled at him sweetly and swam to the other end. As I got out of the pool, I glanced up and saw he was headed in my direction with a mean grin on his face. Suddenly, Presley came around the corner.

"Hey, dude, watch out. I think you're about to step on a scorpion. There were a couple out here earlier. They travel in pairs. Be careful." Peering at the ground by a flower bed Presley yelled, "There goes one right now. Did you see it? I've heard some of them are poisonous."

Turning pale, the red-haired kid turned around and beat a hasty retreat as he headed for his room. Presley looked at me and grinned. Neither one of us said a word. We didn't need to. I thought of that old phrase "comrade in arms." I had never understood exactly what it meant. Now I did.

A woman named Crystal was the new security guard. An attractive, petite blonde, she exuded strength. "Don't let her size fool you," the night clerk told me. "She's tough as a boot. She's retired military on full disability. When she was with the Coast Guard, she got stabbed when she boarded a boat to check for drugs. Then, she was shot five times. Not only did she survive, but she has two grown sons. Crystal doesn't know how to die," he added. "I feel sorry for anyone who tries to educate her in that department."

I was in awe. Finally, one day I got up the courage to talk to her as she sat at the edge of the pool. "Hi, I'm Sophie," I said, extending my hand.

"Hello, Sophie. My name is Crystal."

"Were you really in the Coast Guard? I hear you've been stabbed and have even gotten shot."

"Yes, I was told I'd never walk again, but here I am."

"Did you find it hard dealing with criminals when they're big?" I asked, thinking about the red-headed kid who pushed me into the pool.

"No. A lot of them are cowards. It's a matter of calling their bluffs and letting them know you mean business." Looking at me speculatively, she said, "Would you like it if I taught you some defensive moves? No matter how big some guy is, with the right training, you can take him down."

I was so excited for a minute I couldn't speak. "That would be awesome," I answered.

"I'll meet you on the lawn after you finish your chores tomorrow."

After thanking her profusely, I headed to my room, my feet barely touching the ground. What had started out as a punishment, had become a pleasure. I enjoyed listening to the staff. I had never thought about how hard so many people worked just to get by. I realized the people who worked for the hotel were not only hard working, they were kind and generous.

For the next few days, I met Crystal after she got off work. She taught me things I never would have learned when it came to self-defense. But the best thing of all, she taught me that being small doesn't necessarily mean a person is weak.

Presley was at his best when he played the piano at both lunch and dinner in the dining room. I overheard Charlotte tell Dad that a few people said the reason they checked into the Stagecoach Inn was because they had heard about the kid prodigy who played the piano. "I'm going to be in trouble when he goes to college," she said.

After a hard day's work, Presley and I took a dip in the pool and went to bed early. We got up early, too. We helped guests with their luggage without complaining, no matter how many bags there were. We ran errands and were unfailingly polite. "Why can't you act like the kids who live here?" I heard a woman tell her son who was throwing a tantrum in the lobby.

One day, I walked into my room to find Dad waiting for me. He looked at me thoughtfully for a minute. "Sophie, honey, you look different."

"I do?" I mumbled as I walked toward the closet with Bingo and Bo Jangles on my heels.

"You've changed."

"Really? I don't think I'm any different."

"Yes, you've actually got a tan. That's a first. How well I remember those painful sunburns you used to get. You're taller, and it looks like you're gaining some weight. I love your hair. What have you been doing differently?"

"Nothing. I guess it's just a little longer."

"Well, your mother and I were right. You're lovely, and you're going to be a beauty when you grow up."

Blushing, I ducked my head. "Thanks, Dad," I said as I walked into the bathroom and shut the door. For the first time in my life, I didn't think my dad was just being kind. I did look different, but maybe that was because I was different inside.

I realized Dad was watching me carefully, expecting me to bump into things or stumble and fall. As he had promised, he made an appointment with an eye doctor in Austin. Once we arrived, Dad filled out the paperwork, and I underwent what seemed like an endless array of exams. "Your daughter's vision is 20/20," the doctor told my dad. "She has perfect vision."

"I can't understand it," Dad said. "Her vision has always been bad. She broke her glasses not too long ago, and I thought it would be a real problem. She fell out of a tree recently. Maybe she suffered a mild concussion. Perhaps the fall jarred something in her brain."

"Maybe," the doctor said, although it was obvious, he was skeptical, "but whatever she's doing differently, she needs to keep doing it."

"Told you," I announced once we got back in the car. I didn't say anything further. I knew my vision had improved in the strange world Presley and I had fallen into. I didn't tell Dad we had every intention of going back.

Chapter 22

One morning, we finally got the break we had been waiting for. Dad told me he needed to go to Austin. "There's a new company in Austin, and Charlotte found out they are going to hold a seminar," he said. "Charlotte wants to invite the owners to the hotel, and I want to talk to them about advertising in Texas Trails. We probably won't be back until this evening. Do you think you and Presley will be OK on your own?"

"Of course, Dad. We're not babies."

"All right then," Dad said with a laugh. "You two have been so good lately, if I didn't know better, I'd think you've turned into angels. To tell the truth, it's making me nervous."

When he leaned down and kissed me on the cheek, I felt guilty because I knew he had every right to be nervous. After giving him my most angelic smile, I looked back down at the book I was reading. "He's spending a lot of time with Charlotte," I reflected as I continued to read. "I wonder what that's all about?"

The minute the car pulled out of the parking lot, I rushed outside. After crossing the parking lot, I hurried down a hallway until I came to Presley's room. When he didn't answer the door, I looked down the hall and saw him standing by the Coke machine. "Did you hear the news? Your mom and my dad are on their way to Austin."

"That's right," he replied. "We've got the whole day to ourselves. I just hope we don't get bored."

"I don't think that's going to happen."

Looking at his familiar lopsided grin, freckles, and tousled hair, I couldn't keep from smiling. For a few minutes, we just stood looking at each other. Then, without another word, we ran to the door.

At first, we just stood under the tree staring upward at the canopy of leaves. I hoped Gizmo would appear, but he was nowhere to be seen. Without a word, we both put our hands on the trunk of the tree. I felt nothing at first. Then, my hands began to tingle as I felt a faint pulsing. A few seconds later, I heard something that sounded like a moan. It was as if the tree were talking to me. Startled, I jerked my hand back. When I looked at Presley, I realized he had jerked his hand away, too. His eyes were huge. I think both of us were frightened. Despite being apprehensive, neither one of us was willing to walk away. The tree was calling us, and its allure was irresistible.

"I think my imagination is getting the best of me," Presley said.

"Me, too," I replied. "Shall we do this?"

Presley just nodded his head. We both began to climb. I stopped when it seemed as if the tree had begun to sway. For a minute I thought it was the wind, but there was no wind. Even if there was, the tree was so huge, it would take a gale force to move it.

Again, I began to climb. I stopped again because I could have sworn the bark beneath my hands was moving - almost as if the tree was breathing. "Don't be stupid," I told myself. "Trees don't breathe." It was then I heard a chuckle that seemed to come from within the core of the tree. Was the tree laughing at me? That could not be possible. I thought of my conversation earlier with Amy and her warning that the tree could be haunted. "Superstition," I told myself sternly as I continued to climb. Minutes later, I heard the voice again. It sounded raspy and old. "Presley, did you hear that?"

"I didn't hear anything."

"I did. I'm scared."

"Don't worry. It's probably just the wind."

"Do you think we should climb down and go back inside?"

"We've come this far. Let's not stop now," he said.

Presley was right. We had to continue. It was the only way I would find my mother. Even though she warned us that we should not be in that magic land, I felt once she saw us, she would be so happy I would be able to persuade her to come back to the present world we were now in the process of leaving. The fantasy of a happy reunion with my mother was suddenly interrupted when I heard that raspy sound again. "You're not real," I announced as I continued my climb. "Trees don't breathe."

"Everything alive breathes," the voice croaked. "People are not the only ones who have been given the gift of life. We are alive, too. You humans are too wrapped up in yourselves to believe. All you think about is cutting us down so you can build more and more buildings. If you don't stop, someday the forests will be gone."

Panicked, I almost let go. "Presley, I'm scared. The tree is talking."

Presley looked down at me with a look of astonishment on his face. "I didn't hear a thing."

I felt foolish. "I guess I'm imagining things," I said.

We kept climbing. No matter how high we got, when we looked up, it seemed like we needed to go higher. "I don't remember it taking this long the first time we climbed this tree," I said.

"I don't either."

Finally, we spotted a good-sized branch that could hold the two of us. Inching our way onto it carefully, we crawled out on the limb until we were able to sit down. At first, I just stared out at the canopy of leaves. Then, I glanced down. The Stagecoach Inn looked smaller than a dollhouse. I could see the town of Salado in miniature in the distance. The cars and trucks speeding by on the highway appeared to be so tiny they could have been children's toys.

"This is really cool," Presley said.

"Noted," I said, "but I was hoping we'd find Gizmo."

"He's probably hiding or busy doing his thing, whatever that is. He's probably eating."

Thinking about Gizmo's fascination with food, we both laughed. We had grown to love that silly little guy. I know Presley hoped we'd find him, too.

Gizmo really liked us. If he was here, he would have shown up the minute he heard our voices. "Now that we're here, how are we going to get to that magical kingdom?" I asked, changing the subject.

"Last time we just fell, but at this height, that seems pretty dangerous."

"I know," I responded. "We weren't this high up before. I'm afraid we'll hurt ourselves. We're so high up we could be seriously injured or even killed."

"Maybe we need to move down a little lower."

"You're right," I answered, looking for a lower branch I could reach.

Before I could start my descent, I felt something land on the branch next to me. Because of the leaves, it was hard to see what it was. As I peered through the foliage, I realized it was a crow. Staring into its glittering yellow eyes and seeing its long yellow beak, I watched as it ruffled its feathers. As it danced daintily from one foot to the other, I felt uneasy. I have always liked animals, but there was something about this crow I didn't like. "Caw. Caw. Caw," it screamed as it hopped closer.

"Shoo! Go away," I yelled, trying to swat it away. Darting closer, it pecked my hand. "Ouch," I yelled. "That hurts. Go away you mean, old bird. Get out of here." Glancing behind the ugly bird, I saw another crow approaching Presley. He seemed to be fascinated as he stared at it, but seeing the grim set to his mouth, I realized he was nervous, too.

Not only did the crow next to me refuse to go, but the other crow landed on the branch next to the first. Totally unafraid, both birds tried to peck me. "Go away," I screamed. By now I wasn't trying to swat at the birds. Instead, I was hanging on to the tree for dear life.

"Ouch," I heard Presley yell. He was being pecked at, too. Suddenly, more crows were landing on our branch. All of them were large. As Presley and I tried to keep our balance and shield ourselves from our attackers, I felt the branch begin to move. More birds arrived. All of them seemed intent on doing us harm. The branch was not just moving, it began to bend. Each time we tried to scramble back toward the trunk of the tree, the birds' attacks increased with more of them pecking at our hands and legs. Horrified, I saw blood on Presley's cheek.

"Hang on, Sophie," Presley yelled.

Even as I screamed, I knew no one was there to help us. Just when

I thought things couldn't get worse, I heard a snap as the branch broke. Once again, I was experiencing that sickening sensation of falling. "We'll both be killed," I thought. "This is all my fault. I'll never find my mother, and I'll never see my father again." I was crying as we both fell into a black void.

Part Two

Chapter 1

When I first woke up, I was afraid to open my eyes. Feeling something wet on my face and a slight pressure on my chest, I hoped it was Gizmo. When I finally opened my eyes, Gizmo was nowhere to be seen. Instead, Bingo was licking my face, and Bo Jangles was sitting on my chest.

I could not hear the gentle lapping of waves, the crying of seagulls, or feel the refreshing ocean breeze I had become so familiar with the first time we had fallen out of the tree and landed in prehistoric Texas. Instead, a blazing and unforgiving sun, set in a cloudless sky, was beating down on my face. Every bone in my body ached. Sitting up slowly, I realized I was in the middle of a dirt road – one that had deep, rutted grooves, obviously the result of a heavy vehicle with four wheels. I couldn't see any palm trees. Instead, there were short, stubby trees, shrubs with spines, and maple trees along with box elders, some at least fifty feet tall.

"Sophie, Sophie, are you OK?" Presley called as he ran toward me.

"I'm fine," I replied shakily as I got to my feet. "Where are we?"

"I don't know, but it's not prehistoric Texas. I saw long- horned steers grazing over the hill. Look, there's someone, or something, coming."

At first, all I could make out was a large cloud of dust moving in our direction. We barely had time to jump to the side of the road when a stagecoach pulled by six black horses thundered past. I thought it would continue, but then I heard the driver yell. Pulling on the reins, he skillfully brought the horses to a standstill.

A slim man wearing a black eyepatch, a large red bandana around his neck, and gloves peered down at us from under a wide-brimmed hat. "I wonder why he's wearing gloves in this heat?" I asked myself, still in shock from finding myself in this new setting.

"Where are you two headed?" the stage driver asked. We just stood there; neither one of us knew what to say. "Are you lost?"

Passengers were hanging out the windows and staring at us in astonishment. I realized how strange we must look, Presley in his baggy T-shirt and me in my jean shorts. Feeling a slight burning sensation on my face, I realized I had a sunburn. We were hot, sweaty, and dirty. It was obvious we were millions of years ahead of where we had been the first time we fell out of the tree.

"Yes, sir, we certainly are," Presley said. "We're headed for the Stagecoach Inn in Salado. Could you give us a ride?"

An elderly woman wearing a black bonnet leaned her head out the window and yelled, "They can't ride in here, Charlie. Look how these urchins are dressed. It's indecent. Shame on you," she scolded, directing her irritation at us. "What on earth possessed you to be out here dressed like that?" Jerking her head upward toward the driver, she continued, "We're God-fearing Christians. They have no place with us. Besides, look at that mangy-looking dog and cat. I bet they bite."

I felt a flash of anger toward this rude woman. "Bo Jangles is gorgeous, and Bingo is brave," I almost replied. "I bet you don't even like animals, and I think you're horrid," I wanted to say, but under the circumstances, I decided not to respond.

"Now, Miss Teakins, they are just children. I believe they need help, and I, for one, intend to help them," a soft, feminine voice hidden in the shadows inside the coach said.

Leaning down, the driver extended his hand. "You two can ride up here with me." Moments later, we were sitting next to him with Bingo sitting on Presley's lap and Bo Jangles curled up in my backpack. After the driver flicked his twelve-foot whip over the heads of the horses, we were on our way. At times, the road narrowed until it was little more than a narrow ledge, and one time, we found ourselves hanging on for dear life as the coach lurched and tilted dangerously, careening over an area that was little more than a path strewn with boulders. We were relieved when the road widened and smoothed out. Over the thundering noise of the horses' hooves, the driver shouted, "Where are you two from?"

"I'm from Dallas," I yelled. "Presley is trying to get back to the Stagecoach Inn."

"Dallas is quite a distance. How did you end up in the middle of the road?"

"We fell out of a tree," Presley responded.

After a minute of silence, the driver replied casually, "I see. Well, just to be on the safe side, I want you two checked for injuries by Doc Holliday when we get to the hotel."

As we got closer to the Stagecoach Inn, I was surprised to see groves of pecan and oak trees. "Presley, do you think we're headed to the right place?"

"Yes, I think we're in the 1800s. Things are sure to look a lot different."

"At least we'll be around people," I commented.

"Maybe that's not such a good thing," Presley replied with a thoughtful expression on his face. "According to history, this period was lawless."

As we got closer to the inn, I saw corrals and several outbuildings. Bellowing steers with long, curved horns milled around in one corral. Sheep were in another. When the stagecoach came to a stop in front of the Stagecoach Inn, Presley and I looked at each other in amazement. A sprawling, framed building, it was nothing like the Stagecoach Inn we were familiar with. Cowboys, clad in chaps, boots, and spurs, along with an assortment of travelers, were making their way in and out of the building. I could see women and children chatting on the upstairs veranda. A thin, well-dressed man, who had been sitting in a rocking chair on the porch, stood up and hurried down the steps to help us down.

"Any problems, Charlie?" he asked.

"Nothing to speak of. Things have been pretty quiet. Word must be out that the iron box holding the gold and silver bullion is nailed to the floor," Charlie said as he swung two large mailbags to the ground.

"You always manage to get the mail and gold through, Charlie. You're the best stagecoach driver in the state."

"Luck, I guess," Charlie said as he helped us down.

"I'd call it skill. Who are these kids?"

"Don't know, Doc. Found them in the middle of the road about three miles from here. They say they fell out of a tree. The girl says she's from Dallas. The boy claims he lives here."

Just then a woman stepped out of the coach and rushed to our side. "Children, you are obviously in trouble. The first thing we need to do is get you some decent clothes."

Speechless, Presley and I could only stare at her in amazement. She was the same beautiful woman wearing the same black-and-white plaid silk dress we had seen in the vision while in the tree during our return from prehistoric Texas. She was even wearing the same hat with the jaunty feather. The coach door slammed open again. Out jumped the same little girl and young boy we also had seen in that same vision. Rushing to the beautiful woman's side, their mouths were hanging open as they stared at us.

"Children, it's rude to stare. Mind your manners."

"Holy Jeepers," the boy exclaimed. "What happened to you? Were you attacked by Indians? Did they take your clothes?"

"Uh, no," Presley said. I could almost hear the wheels turning in his head. We both realized that just as people in the modern world we came from didn't believe us, it was doubtful people in this world would believe us once they heard our story.

"All we remember is that we fell out of a tree," I announced.

A pretty, teenage girl joined the small group that had gathered around us. She, too, was the same girl we had seen in the vision.

"I have an extra dress you can have," she said, looking at me. "We can cut it down to your size. My name is Hayley. This is my brother Tom, my sister Isadora, and my Aunt Elizabeth."

"Thanks. My name is Sophie, and this is Presley."

"Are you brother and sister?"

"No, we're best friends," Presley replied.

"He plays the piano," I interjected. "He's a musical genius."

"Before anyone does anything, I need to check these two over for injuries," Doc announced.

"Are you a pediatrician?" Seeing the blank looks on the faces of those around me, I realized that word in this world had no meaning. "I mean a children's doctor," I added hastily.

"Even though I'm a dentist, I fill a lot of needs around here," Doc Holliday responded.

Before I could think of anything else to say, he started to cough. Pulling a handkerchief out of his pocket, he covered his mouth. The coughing didn't stop. It went on and on as he struggled to breathe. Finally, it did stop but not before I noticed two tiny spots of blood on the handkerchief he hastily put back into his pocket.

Just then, the door of the hotel opened and a heavyset woman with a prominent nose and dressed in what could best be described as a "dance-hall" costume, rushed to Doc Holliday's side. "Get in here, Doc," she fussed, grabbing his arm. "You need to sit down and take a breather."

"Follow me, young 'uns," Doc said over his shoulder as he was being propelled through the door. "This is Kate, and she can get mad as hops if I don't do what she says."

"Who are these kids?" Kate asked the doctor once we were inside.

"I don't know. Both are talking a lot of flap doodle. Something about falling out of a tree. They've either suffered concussions, or they are telling fibs. I need to check them out and make sure they don't have any injuries."

After sitting down on the red velvet Victorian sofa in the lobby, I opened my backpack. Bo Jangles jumped down, stretched, and immediately lay across my feet. Bingo flopped down on the floor. They both seemed indifferent to the hubbub around us. Miss Elizabeth, Tom, Isadora, and Hayley watched as we sat patiently while Doc Holliday examined us.

"No injuries that I can see," he said after he finished poking and prodding us. "As far as I can tell, you two are perfectly healthy. Tell me again how you found yourselves in the middle of the road. If you're lying, that's not a good idea – especially around here. Who are your parents?"

"My mother disappeared. I'm hoping I can find her," I answered, "and we're not lying."

"I just wanted to come home, but this is not what I remember. And we did fall out of a tree," Presley added.

"That's all we remember," I said again as I crossed my fingers behind my back. "Lie number one," I thought to myself. "I hope there won't be too many more."

The delicious aroma of something cooking floated across the lobby. Hearing my stomach growl, I realized I was hungry. I was sure Presley was, too. Remembering his sophistication when it came to dining, I wasn't surprised when he asked if we could see a menu.

"No menu in these parts," Doc Holliday laughed. "You eat what you get. It's announced daily, but we have a new cook, and things are really looking up. Breakfast used to consist of beef jerky, crackers, onions, and bacon. Dinner was pan fried venison and antelope. This new cook is a marvel. Her pot pies, steaks, bread, hush puppies, and cobblers are the talk of the county."

"How much is dinner?" Presley asked.

"Twenty-five cents."

Looking at each other, Presley and I realized this was a problem. A meal for twenty-five cents in the world we came from was unheard of. Even so, it could have been five cents, and it wouldn't matter because neither one of us had a penny.

Seeing the looks on our faces, Miss Elizabeth put an arm around each of us. "Don't worry, children. For the time being, I'm buying your meals. Until we sort things out, you'll be staying with us."

"Aunt Elizabeth just got hired as the teacher," Tom said. "People are cleaning out the school cabin and building an extra one for us. Until then, we get to stay at the hotel."

"Where's your parents?" I asked.

"Killed by Indians," was the sad reply.

Just then Kate swept into the room. "I heard you play the piano," she said, looking at Presley intently.

"Yes, Ma'am, I do."

"If you're any good, you can play a couple nights a week for our guests. Your meals will be on us."

"I would be delighted, Ma'am."

"Just a darn minute. Let's make sure you can keep your end of the bargain. I want to hear you play," Miss Kate insisted.

Within minutes, Presley was sitting on a piano stool facing an old upright piano. Bo Jangles jumped to the top of the piano. With his head hanging over the top, he looked down expectantly at the keys. As for Bingo, he sat quietly at Presley's side.

"Will you look at that?" I heard someone say. "Those critters act like they own the place. Have you ever seen a funnier looking dog?"

"Nope. It's no herd dog, that's for sure."

I was concerned as I remembered Presley's shiny black baby grand piano in the world we came from.

"I think we've got some sheet music around here somewhere," Miss Kate said.

"No problem," Presley replied with a grin on his face. "I've got this."

Just like the guests of the hotel in modern times, within minutes, the audience was spellbound. Cowboys and passengers alike came into the dining room as Presley's fingers flew over the keyboard. It wasn't long before there was a crowd. He played classical music, ragtime, and to my amazement, even some old Western favorites. Isadora, wearing the same white dress with the blue-ribbon sash I remembered, was dancing around the room, lost in her own world of make believe. There were even a couple of Native Americans in the crowd. Their faces showed no emotion, but I heard one say as he turned to the other, "White boy has spirit fingers. Mighty powerful magic."

I saw tears in the eyes of some and wide smiles on the faces of others. When he stopped, everyone started clapping and stamping their feet.

"Kid, that was amazing," Miss Kate announced. "Some of it I've never heard before, but I like it and so do they," she said as she pointed at the crowd. "I don't know who you are or where you came from, but you don't ever have to worry about a meal in this establishment as long as I run things. Let's get both of you a decent meal."

With that, we were ushered into the dining room. With everyone talking at once, we sat at a large table along with Miss Elizabeth, Haley, Tom, and Isadora. Every few minutes, people would stop by the table to congratulate Presley. When someone started questioning us about where we were from, Miss Elizabeth would give them a warning look and change the subject. The food was delicious. Homemade bread, pickles, fried okra, and a chicken casserole that was followed by a blueberry cobbler was some of the most delicious food I've ever eaten. When no one was looking, I handed tidbits of food under the table to Bingo and Bo Jangles.

Later, I overheard Aunt Elizabeth talking to Doc Holliday. "I think these children are sincere," she said. "It's evident they've had a shock of some kind, and they are traumatized. It was weeks after Tom and Isadora's parents were killed before they could remember a thing. We need to be patient. I'm sure their memories will come back eventually. More than likely, they're just too painful to deal with."

"Damfino," ("damned if I know") Doc Holliday responded with a shrug of his shoulders. "I'll leave them to you. The sheriff just informed me I'm under house arrest. He has ordered me to stay in my room indefinitely."

"Gun fighting again?"

"Damned Horn Swaggler. He was cheating at cards, and when I caught him, he challenged me to a duel."

"Is that why you had to leave Dallas?"

"No. I had an office downtown in that fair city, but I couldn't stop coughing. It made my patients nervous."

"Consumption is no laughing matter, Doc. You need to take care of yourself."

With that they left the room, and I was left to wonder. Thinking back to Doc's coughing and the flecks of blood on his handkerchief, I realized his consumption was more than likely tuberculosis. With no antibiotics or modern medicines, Doc's death was inevitable. Even though I barely knew him, I felt sad.

As Hayley and Tom led us up to their hotel room, I saw Miss Kate facing a large man who was wearing a badge in the hallway.

"I can't believe you're confining Doc to his room," she shouted.

"He's lucky I don't put him in jail. He's a gambler and a killer. That man barely got his gun out of his holster before Doc shot him dead in broad daylight. In my opinion, it wasn't a fair fight."

"The man tried to cheat him in a card game."

"Maybe so, but Doc is too quick to draw his guns."

"When do you plan to let him out? He's helped a lot of people with their ailments, and he's well liked. He's not well himself."

"That's exactly why I'm confining him to his room. Can't have the town in an uproar. You can take him his meals, but I plan to send a telegram to Dallas to see if he has any outstanding warrants. Meanwhile, he can cool his heels here."

Miss Kate turned on her heel and marched down the hall.

When we opened the door to what was now our hotel room, we could only stand still for a minute and gaze at our surroundings. The decor looked like something out of a Western movie. The wallpaper sported large, pink cabbage roses and vines on a rich green background. There was a wash basin and pitcher on a stand along with a double-globed lamp, a brass bed, and a wardrobe. Lace curtains hung in the windows, and a door opened onto a veranda. Bo Jangles and Bingo immediately jumped up on the beds and went to sleep. Holding my breath, I waited for our hosts to shoo them out, but Isadora, Tom, and even Miss Elizabeth, after staring at them in amazement, burst out laughing. "Looks like we've got a couple more residents in this room," Miss Elizabeth announced.

Within minutes, Presley had changed into some of Tom's clothes. When Miss Elizabeth started pulling dresses out of the wardrobe, Tom announced he was going to show Presley around town. After they left, I tried on two dresses. Miss Elizabeth and Hayley, after cutting into the fabric and applying a series of tiny, neat stitches, made the dresses fit me perfectly. "I couldn't do that if my life depended on it," I thought wistfully, thinking back to my pitiful attempts at embroidery. Then, Hayley pulled a pair of high-topped leather shoes out of the wardrobe. Even though they showed signs of wear, I knew in this world, they were probably a precious commodity. "Take these," she said, holding them out to me. "I don't need them. They pinch my toes." Moved, I didn't know what to say.

A few hours later, Hayley and I were walking slowly hand in hand down the boardwalk. Catching my reflection in the hardware store window, I stopped. With short blonde, curly hair adorned with a blue ribbon and a body clad in a long, cotton dress, the girl staring back at me could have been a typical teenager born and raised in the 1800s. She even looked happy.

Hours later, Presley and I were on the floor tucked into pallets that had been made up of pillows and blankets. Bingo lay at Presley's feet, and Bo Jangles, after giving me a kiss on my cheek, positioned himself on the pillow next to my head. His vibrating purr was hypnotic. It had been a very long day. Even though we had fallen from one world into another, we were still in the same location – the Stagecoach Inn in Salado. However, this time we were in a time that Presley referred to as the Wild West. "I don't think it's so wild," I thought sleepily. "These people are nice. If we can convince them we're telling the truth, maybe they can help me find my mother." With that, I fell into a deep and dreamless sleep.

A few hours later, I jerked awake. I could hear yelling, screaming, and the sounds of people running in the hall.

"What's happening?" Presley yelled.

"Fire," someone shouted.

Chapter 2

As Presley and I peered out the window, we saw total chaos. Flames were shooting upward, lighting up the black sky. A shed was on fire, and it was dangerously close to the hotel.

"Come, children. We need to get out of the hotel. If that fire spreads, we could be next," Miss Elizabeth instructed as she shoved clothes and papers into a carpet bag. Once we coaxed Bingo and Bo Jangles out from under the bed, I put Bo Jangles in my backpack, and Presley attached the leash to Bingo before tucking him under his arm. We rushed into the hallway, made our way down the stairs, and ran out the door where we joined a growing crowd watching the fire from the road. A brigade of customers and employees alike had already formed a line as they passed buckets of water from the well to the burning building. It was then I heard a scream.

"Did you hear that, Presley? That voice sounds familiar."

"Yes," Presley replied as he handed Bingo to a startled cowboy. I shrugged off my backpack, and within seconds, we were running toward the shed.

"Get back here you darn kids," someone yelled. "You'll get your fool selves killed."

After racing inside, we couldn't see anything at first because of the smoke. When it cleared briefly, I saw a tall, slender figure tied to a post. It was Amy. Rivulets of tears and sweat had left ashy trails on her face. Eyes wide with terror, she was trying desperately to get loose. Amy is strong, but the thick ropes around her bleeding wrists were too tight, even for her.

"Help me," she screamed. "I don't want to die."

"We'll save you. We won't let you die." My eyes were streaming, and even though I tried to sound confident, my voice was shaking.

Presley grabbed a nearby board and began applying pressure between the post and rope that bound her wrists, hoping to loosen the rope.

"This isn't working," he yelled. "Can you find something else?"

Stumbling to a shelf on the wall, I ran my hands over the dirty surface until I felt something sharp prick my fingers. It was a rusty knife. Grabbing the handle, I rushed back to the post, and while Presley continued to apply pressure, I attempted to cut the rope. Momentarily forgetting that I had decided I didn't believe in God, I prayed. "Please, God, help us. Amy is my friend. Don't let her die."

Progress seemed agonizingly slow as I sawed through the rope strand by strand. Finally, the last strand parted, and Amy was free. Because she was too weak to stand, Presley and I each grabbed an arm and began dragging her toward the door. We found ourselves struggling because of Amy's height as we slowly inched our way forward. I screamed when a burning rafter, accompanied by a shower of sparks, crashed directly behind us.

"Keep going and don't look back," Presley yelled. We barely had time to throw ourselves out the door when the roof, accompanied by burning debris, collapsed. We had made it out just in time.

Seconds later, people rushed forward and dragged us away from the flames. Two of the hotel employees laid Amy gently on the grass and began checking her for injuries. "I'll be alright," I heard her say, her voice weak.

"Children, are you alright?" Miss Elizabeth asked with a worried look on her face as she began checking us for injuries. Both of us could barely stand. Presley was leaning on Tom, and Isadora had wrapped her arms around my waist.

"You two are bricks," Tom announced, looking at us with admiration. "That was the bravest thing I've ever seen."

"I thought you were going to die," Isadora wailed.

"We're fine," I assured her. Being an only child, I had often yearned for a little sister. It was at that moment I decided if I could have had one, I would have wanted her to be just like Isadora.

After the fire was out, leaving nothing behind but a smoldering ruin, we were escorted back into the hotel. By this time, Amy was able to walk. Covered with bruises, the only serious damage was the rope burns on her wrists.

"Where's Doc?" I heard someone ask.

Unusually quiet, Miss Kate came into the room carrying a large basin of water along with sponges and bandages. When she handed them to Miss Elizabeth, she could barely look at us. Just then, the sheriff came in.

"Doc is gone. Did you set that fire, Kate?"

"Wherever did you get a fool notion like that? I have no idea what you are talking about."

"Mighty convenient that Doc has disappeared. That fire was quite a diversion."

Crouching down, he stared at Amy who was sitting quietly while Kate was bandaging her wrists.

"Where did you come from, and how did you get tied up in that shed."

"I was looking for Sophie and Presley. I fell out of the tree."

The sheriff stared at her in stunned silence. "That tree again?" he yelled. "Where in the hell is that tree these kids say they keep falling out of? I've a mind to cut the damned thing down."

"It's in the courtyard," I interjected meekly, "but it can't be the same tree because it's too small."

After looking at me in disbelief and shaking his head, the sheriff turned his attention back to Amy.

"Girl, you from a plantation around here?"

"No. I'm from Dallas."

"You know these two?"

"Yes, Sophie is my friend. I decided to follow her so I can help Sophie find her mother."

"How did you end up tied to that post."

"I was on the road when two men grabbed me," she sobbed. "They said I was a runaway slave. I tried to tell them I wasn't, but they just laughed. They knocked me down and began hitting and kicking me. Then they tied me to a rope and made me run behind their horses until they got to the shed. I begged them to let me go, but they said they'd find my owner and collect a bounty. They said I'd get a whipping and probably get a foot broken so I couldn't run again. Then, they tied me to the post inside the shed and left. I was there for hours. When the fire broke out, I thought I was going to die."

"Damned fools," the sheriff snarled. "The war's over. All of the black folk are free."

"Yes, but a lot of them don't know that, and their former masters are not about to tell them," a grim-faced Miss Kate said.

Looking sorrowfully at Amy, she patted her face. "I am so sorry, dear," she whispered. "I would never have forgiven myself if you had been hurt, or worse yet, died. I hope I can make it up to you."

"Can you describe those two meaters (cowards)?" the sheriff asked Amy.

"It was hard to see because it was dark, but I heard one call the other one Sugar Foot."

Miss Kate and the sheriff exchanged a meaningful glance, one that spoke volumes.

"Should have known it," the sheriff said. "It's Harris Moore."

"Why do people call him Sugar Foot?" I asked.

"Not only is he a bungler, he's a coward. He started small, robbing homesteads and unaware individuals, but it looks like he's moving on to bigger things. The last I heard, he's teamed up with Black Bart. They're robbing trains."

Looking at Amy with compassion, he patted her on the knee. "Don't worry, girl. I'll catch him. He came west to be a cowboy, but he's so damn clumsy that he earned his nickname honestly. He'll make a mistake. He always does."

After the sheriff left, we were too excited to go to bed, so we headed to the dining room where Miss Kate cooked up eggs, bacon, and biscuits.

"Where can I stay?" Amy asked.

"We'll make another pallet on the floor," Miss Elizabeth answered. Rolling her eyes and laughing, she added, "After all, what's one more?"

Minutes later, I jerked up. The excitement had worn off, and I had started to doze off while still sitting at the table. I have never been so exhausted. Thanking Miss Kate for the meal, we trailed up the stairs. In minutes, Miss Elizabeth had arranged another pallet on the floor. I had to stifle a giggle when Amy lay down because her feet protruded out from under the blanket. Bingo went back under the bed, and Bo Jangles moved onto my pillow positioning himself next to my head. The last thing I remember was looking over at Presley. He was sound asleep. "He really is amazing," I thought, before drifting off.

Chapter 3

The next morning, I awoke to the trill of singing birds. It sounded like they were putting on a full-scale musical event, each one trying to outdo the other. "There's nothing like birds singing to lift one's spirits," I thought. Then my mind drifted back to the crows that caused Presley and me to fall out of the tree when we were trying to get back to prehistoric Texas. Pushing that scary memory out of my mind, I focused on the sound of wagons, muted voices, and horses, all on the road below. Feeling refreshed, I jumped up, opened the window, and looked outside. It was a beautiful day. Overhearing snatches of words, I realized many of the men and women were talking about last night's fire. "Did you hear about that poor black girl who was tied up inside the shed?" one man asked.

"Yep. Pretty dang mean if you ask me. Just hope they find those rat bags. Heard one of them is Sugar Foot. Hanging's too good for him."

As I turned away from the window Amy was unwinding herself from her blankets. When she stood up, she was wearing a pair of Ms. Elizabeth's pantaloons and a cotton, laced top. The pantaloons only reached the middle of her legs, and the laced top showed a good portion of her torso. I covered my mouth to keep from laughing. "Now what am I going to do?" she demanded, looking at me with disgust. "You have no idea how hard it is being this tall."

"You're beautiful, Amy," I said, feeling contrite. "I believe you're going to be a model when you grow up."

"I don't think I'll find too many modeling jobs around here," she replied.

Just then, we heard a knock on the door. When I opened it, there was a package wrapped in brown paper and tied in string on the floor next to a pair of cowboy boots. Carrying everything inside, I pulled out the note and read, "Amy, I think these clothes will fit you, and I found the cowboy boots in a closet. The owner is long gone or dead. I think they're your size." It was signed, "Your friend, Kate."

Amy's eyes lit up as she opened the package. It contained a long dark blue skirt and blouse that looked almost new. Kate was right. The boots were a perfect fit.

"A lot of people here are nice," I ventured, "not including those creeps who kidnapped you."

"There's bad people everywhere. My mother told me that. You're right about one thing. People here are nice, but why is Miss Kate being extra nice to me?"

"Doc Holliday was here until last night. Now he's disappeared. The sheriff was mad at him, and he was confined to his hotel room because he got in a duel and killed a man who tried to cheat him at cards. Miss Kate was furious because I suspect she loves Doc. I'm pretty sure she set the shed on fire to create a diversion so Doc could get away. He's probably on his way to Tombstone where he'll join his friend Wyatt Earp. She had no idea you were inside. I can tell she feels terrible. I'm so glad you're OK."

"Yes, thanks to you and Presley. You saved my life."

I crossed the room and hugged her. "If there was ever anyone who deserved to be saved, it's you."

"Don't kid yourself. I could have been a total stranger, and you and Presley still would have rushed into that burning building. That's just what you do."

Not knowing how to respond, I said, "Let's sit outside on the veranda until the others get up." Minutes later, we were sitting in rocking chairs, enjoying the clean air, sunshine, and growing bustle in the street below. "This may not be as exotic as prehistoric Texas," I said, "but it's still pretty neat."

Amy looked over at me and smiled. "I know you didn't expect to end up here. Even though it's not the prehistoric Texas you told me about, you must admit, it's got its own peculiar charm. I'm just glad we didn't arrive while the Civil War was going on."

"Amy, why did you come? Your mother told you the tree was dangerous."

"Yes, but the elders also said you needed to climb it again so you could find answers to your mom's disappearance. I decided I wanted to help."

"It may have been a huge mistake, but I'm glad you're here. When I realized it was you in that burning shed, I was so terrified, I even prayed."

"I thought you didn't believe in God."

"I don't, but when I think back to how we got out of that shed just in time, it seems like a miracle. Now, I'm really confused."

"Don't worry," Amy replied with a dazzling smile. "You'll figure it out."

As she rocked back and forth, she began softly singing a song in an African dialect. I had no idea what the words meant but found them strangely comforting.

Chapter 4

Later that day, I was surprised to see the sheriff headed our way.

"Charlie is taking the mail along with a gold and silver shipment to Round Rock to be put on the train," he said. "That trip takes a full day, Kate has fixed a picnic lunch. I've wired ahead. I want all three of you to go with him."

Turning to Amy, he continued, "When you get there, I want you to talk to the sheriff and tell him what happened when you were kidnapped. He might have an idea where Sugar Foot and Black Bart are hanging out."

Looking at Presley and me, he added, "Remember anything about your folks?"

Crossing my fingers behind my back, I replied, "No, sir, not a thing."

"Me neither," Presley quickly added.

"Well, maybe someone there has heard something. You better find Charlie. He's about ready to leave."

"What room is he in?"

"Charlie never stays in a room. He bunks in the stable."

Upon hearing this, I picked up Bo Jangles, and Presley grabbed Bingo before we rushed out the door. When we reached the stable, Charlie had just finished feeding the last of his six black horses. Talking to them tenderly, he led them outside where he began hitching them up to the stagecoach.

"Why do you sleep in the stable?" I asked.

"My horses are better company than most people," was the polite but terse response.

I considered asking him why he always wore gloves but decided against it.

After loading up the mail sacks and securing the iron money box to the floor, he said, "You two are welcome to ride inside, but I think if I were you and had my druthers, I'd rather ride up-side with me."

I knew instinctively Presley would prefer riding on top with Charlie and so would I, but I was curious.

"We'd love to ride up-side with you, but why do you think we'd prefer riding on top?"

"I only have two passengers. One of them is going to visit her sister in Round Rock. I don't think you'd enjoy her company."

"Who is she?"

"The Widow Teakins."

I couldn't help but notice Charlie's grin when he saw the expressions of dismay on our faces. "I'd rather run behind the coach all the way to Round Rock just to be as far as possible from that mean old woman," I fumed as I climbed aboard. Since there wasn't enough room on top, Amy had to ride inside.

When Charlie steered the coach to the front of the hotel, Miss Teakins took one look at us and shook her head in disgust. When she saw Amy, I thought she was going to cancel her trip. With her mouth set in a grim line, she finally allowed Charlie to help her inside. "Those brats again?" I heard her mutter.

Next came Mr. Olson, who was a portly man, wearing a pin-striped suit with a gold watch attached to the lapel. Tipping his hat to us, he stepped inside the coach.

Minutes later, we were on our way. By now, Presley and I weren't surprised by the twists and turns of a road that at times seemed to disappear, causing the coach to careen around sharp turns. I was sure it was Charlie's skill with his whip and his understanding of his horses that not only kept the stagecoach from turning over, it also kept us from falling into a ravine.

The road had just leveled out when, without warning, two figures jumped out of the bush into the middle of the road, forcing Charlie to bring the horses to a halt. Both wore bandanas over their faces. With guns drawn, one of them yelled, "Throw down that lock box."

"Can't, you damned fool. It's bolted to the floor."

"Unbolt it or forfeit your life."

One of the bandits yanked open the door and stuck his gun in Miss Teakins' face. "Get out of the coach, you old biddy, and put your hands in the air."

Instead of being afraid, the widow, with her jaw thrust forward and eyes blazing, yelled, "You'll hang for this."

The other bandit, while keeping one eye on Charlie, peered inside the stagecoach where Amy was cowering in the farthest corner. "Lookee who we got here, Sugar Foot. It's our little friend."

"You mean that tall drink of water slave girl we left tied up in the shed, Black Bart? Hoped we'd meet up with her again. We'll take her with us. Even though we can't sell her in Texas, we're sure to get a good price for her in Mexico."

Once the passengers were outside the coach, Black Bart tried to grab the widow's purse. Refusing to let go, she hung on for dear life. After a few minutes, Black Bart hit her on the side of her head with his pistol. Without a word, she slumped to the ground. White-faced, Mr. Olson stood silently with his hands in the air as Sugar Foot yanked the gold watch out of his lapel.

Suddenly, without warning, Bingo jumped off the coach and latched onto one of Sugar Foot's pant legs, sinking his teeth into his ankle. At the same time, Bo Jangles let out a deep growl and took a flying leap, sinking his claws and teeth into Black Bart's neck.

The brief distraction was all Charlie needed. He snapped his whip over the horses' heads, causing them to bolt. Just as Sugar Foot fired off a shot, Charlie lashed him across his face with his whip. Intent on escape, Black Bart leaped onto his horse, but he didn't get far. Charlie, after taking careful aim with his shotgun, fired, filling Bart's backside with buck shot. The last we saw, Black Bart was slumped over in his saddle as his horse galloped down the road.

Clamoring down, Presley and I first rushed to Amy who was sitting on the ground and looking dazed. "You better tend to Miss Teakins," she said with a worried look on her face.

The unconscious widow was lying in a heap of black skirt and petticoats. Her hat and veil had fallen off, and her gray hair had fallen in tangles around her face. The contents of the purse she had clung to so desperately were scattered all over the ground. With the help of Mr. Olson, Presley lifted her head and eased a few drops of water into her mouth. As her eyes fluttered open, she looked confused. Then, as the memory of the attempted robbery resurfaced, she looked frightened.

"Don't be afraid," Presley said. "They're gone. Charlie hit the one called Sugar Foot with his whip. I think he blinded him. He shot the other one called Black Bart. From the looks of it, I don't think he'll get far."

Meanwhile, I was gathering the widow's belongings and putting them back in her purse. Seeing a tin poking out of the nearby weeds, I held it up to read the lettering. I was surprised to see it was snuff. I'm sure no one suspected that this proper Christian lady had a vice. She chewed tobacco. When she saw me with the tin in my hand, she yelled, "Put that in my purse this instant and bring it over here right now." When I handed the purse to her, she announced in a huff, "Well, I never!" As Presley helped her up, I turned away, not wanting her to see my smile.

Presley and I then cautiously approached Sugar Foot, who was lying in a heap on the ground. When Presley pushed him over with his foot, Sugar Foot had Mr. Olson's gold watch clutched in one hand. He was dead.

"What do we do now, Charlie? Do we just leave him here?" I yelled.

"No, there's rope and a tarp inside the coach. Get Mr. Olson to help you. Wrap him up and tie him onto the back of the coach."

Surprised that Charlie was still sitting on top of the stagecoach, I looked up. To my dismay, I saw that he was cradling one hand against his chest as blood pooled onto his coat.

"Presley," I yelled, "come quick! Charlie's been shot."

Chapter 5

Mr. Olson, Presley, and I eased Charlie down from his seat and helped him over to the base of a willow tree where it was cool.

I began to cry. "Charlie, please don't die."

"Don't cry, Miss Sophie. I have been hurt a lot worse than this. The bullet went straight through my arm. It didn't even hit the bone. Sugar Foot always was a lousy shot. Lucky for me, that gib face never could do anything right."

Without a word, Widow Teakins lifted her skirt and began tearing strips of cloth off her petticoat. The cranky woman I disliked was gone, replaced by a woman who was as efficient as a nurse on a battlefield. "Take these, girlie," she ordered. "Help Charlie take off his coat. Mr. Olson, you take that bucket off the back of the coach and go down to the creek and fetch some water. That wound needs to be cleaned."

Turning to Presley, she instructed, "Young man, don't just stand there. Make yourself useful. Gather some firewood. You need to build a fire."

Then, without a word she collapsed, sliding down to the ground.

Amy rushed to her side. "She's fainted."

"Not surprised," Charlie said weakly. "She's in worse shape than me. I can already see a lump forming on her head. That was a nasty blow that meater (coward) dealt her. The poor woman cannot breathe. Miss Amy, would you help the Widow Teakins into the coach so she can lie down?"

Once Amy got the Widow Teakins into the coach, she loosened the stays of her corset before joining me.

While Presley was looking for wood, and Mr. Olson had gone to the creek, Amy and I helped Charlie ease out of his coat. When I noticed blood had soaked into his gloves, I eased them off gently. For the first time, I saw his hands. It was then I understood why he always wore gloves. The narrow palms and long dainty fingers were not those of a man. They were the hands of a woman. As Amy and I looked at Charlie in surprise, he gazed wordlessly back at us. "You've found me out. You're the only ones who know."

"We won't tell anyone but Presley," I said. "We don't keep secrets from each other, but first we need to know why."

When Mr. Olson brought back the bucket from the creek, Charlie asked him to check on the widow. "Miss Teakins was hit hard. Please put a compress on her head and sit with her to make sure she's all right."

Without a word, Mr. Olson headed for the coach.

As Amy and I cleaned and bound Charlie's wound, we realized he was right. The bullet had gone all the way through his arm.

"We may have to spend the night, Charlie," Presley said when he returned. "It's late, and I think the injury to your arm will make it too difficult to drive."

"Nope, we'll sit here for a little bit. I need to get the mail and gold and silver bullion to Round Rock. Once we get going, you can hold the reins, and I'll help you."

Amy and I were not alone in noticing Charlie's hands. After looking at them carefully, Presley looked at me. Even though he did not say a word, it was obvious he knew Charlie's secret.

"You're right about the widow," Mr. Olson yelled from inside the coach. "She's not feeling well. I'm staying in here with her."

"I want to know who you really are Charlie," I said.

Spellbound, we listened as Charlie, after leaning his head back against the tree, told his story.

"My real name is Charlotte Parkhurst. My mother was a wonderful person. My pa drank, and when he got drunk, he got mean. He beat my poor ma, and no one lifted a finger to help her. Then, she got sick, but as far as I am concerned, she worked herself to death. When she died,

Pa took off. My brother and I ended up in an orphanage. We rarely got a decent meal. Looking back, we orphans were slave labor. I was a rebellious kid, so I got a lot of beatings. It didn't take long to realize boys have advantages over girls. When a boy speaks his mind, people say he's got courage. Girls, on the other hand, are expected to be meek and mild-mannered."

"What about your mother's family? Didn't she have friends?" I asked.

"Her family never approved of the marriage, so they disowned her. People were slow to make friends with her because she was from the East. They thought she was too highfalutin' because of the way she talked and dressed. What few friends she did have, Pa ran off. The neighbors were afraid of him."

"I knew I'd have to leave the orphanage when I was eighteen," Charlie continued. "There are only two paths open for women - get married or work in a saloon catering to every drunk who walks in the door. Orphans are looked down on, so more than likely, if I got married, it would be to someone poor. Even if I managed to marry a man of means, I'd be under his thumb. That wouldn't work for me. I've always been too independent."

As she talked, Charlie went on to point out other disadvantages women in this world were subject to.

"Ever wondered why the death rate for women is so high? Take fashion, for instance. The smaller a woman's waist, the more feminine she is thought to be, so women wear those danged corsets. Made of whale bone, some of those contraptions weigh thirty pounds. There are fainting couches in gathering places because it's a common thing for women to swoon. That adds to the myth that women are the weaker sex. They faint because they can't breathe. Then there are the contraptions worn under their hoop skirts. It's not unusual for a woman to catch fire when she accidentally brushes against a candle. Those petticoats, hoops, and skirts make a fine torch. If a woman's lucky and the fire is put out, she's only burnt, but more times than not, she dies."

Presley, Amy, and I sat in total silence. I had admired the elegant and beautifully crafted clothing I had seen women wear since we arrived. "I will never admire these fashions again," I decided.

"Take the Widow Teakins," Charlie continued, looking toward the coach. "She's a tough one, but did you notice how she fell to the ground shortly after she seemed like she was on the mend? It was because of that damn corset she's wearing along with the high-collared, tight-necked shirt with mutton sleeves that are tucked into a skirt that drags on the ground. Notice how pale a lot of women are? That's due to those ads in the paper touting tonics that claim if women buy their snake oil, they are guaranteed to have beautiful complexions. The trouble is that a lot of that snake oil contains arsenic. After a time, it can kill them. At the same time, women are expected to haul water, take care of children, and cook."

As Charlie continued her story, I realized life in the 1800s was not only difficult for women, it could be dangerous. Thinking about the freedom my mother and others like her enjoyed in the modern world, I was glad I had been born in the 21st century.

"As a woman, once married, I'd be expected to have a lot of children," Charlie said. "Some women have a baby every year, and a lot of women die in childbirth. Once I did get married, if I didn't have children, people would pity me. Ain't it strange that women are considered the weaker sex? Some folks even believe we have feeble minds."

"How did you manage to disguise yourself and fool everybody?" Presley asked.

"When I was fifteen, I made up my mind I'd never be any man's broodmare or slave. One night, I swiped a boy's clothes and took off. I walked and hitched rides on wagons for three days. On the third day, I came to a town and hid in the stable. I was so hungry I was eating out of the oat bag meant for the horses. When the stable boss caught me, it didn't take him long to figure out that I was pretending to be a boy. I begged him not to turn me in."

"What happened?" I asked.

"After he found out I was an orphan, he decided to help me. He taught me how to walk and talk like a man, chew tobacco, and cuss. I've always had a liking for animals. When he saw how well I worked with horses, he taught me how to handle a team."

"What happened to your eye?" Amy asked.

"I got kicked by a horse. I learned the hard way you can't rush them. You've heard the term 'horse sense'? There's a reason for that. They're smarter than a lot of people, and like people, they all have different personalities. That particular horse was old and cranky, and she showed me who was boss when I got impatient."

After staying silent for a few minutes Charlie said, "Now you know my story. Appreciate it if you don't tell anyone. I'll be your friend for life."

Filled with admiration, I was so moved at first, I couldn't speak. "I'll never tell a soul," I promised. "Cross my heart and hope to die."

"Me neither," Presley said as Amy nodded silently. "You don't have to worry about us. We always keep our promises."

Charlie's face lit up, and he gave us a dazzling smile. Seeing that smile, I realized that the grown-up Charlene would have been a raving beauty. It was sad that to survive, she had to take on the persona of a man. I felt grateful knowing that no matter what, I could always be myself, but I was confused.

"I don't know what to call you," I said. "Should I call you Charlene?"

"No. That girl is long gone. She died and became a boy in every respect at the age of fifteen. In my heart and soul, I am a man. Think of me that way, and always call me Charlie."

Amy, Presley, and I stared at Charlie for a minute. "We will," we said in unison.

Charlie leaned his head against the trunk of the tree and closed his eyes. "Feeling better already," he announced.

A short time later, with Amy back in the coach with the widow and Mr. Olson, we were on our way. Presley, with guidance from Charlie, was handling the reins. Seeing the wide grin on his face as the team of horses galloped down the road, I realized this was an experience he would cherish for the rest of his life.

Two hours later, we pulled up to the courthouse in Round Rock. Sheriff Egan, surrounded by a group of grim-faced men, was waiting for us on the courthouse steps.

Chapter 6

"What happened, Charlie?" the sheriff asked when he saw Presley sitting in the driver's seat next to Charlie who was clasping the blood-stained sleeve of his coat.

"Sugar Foot and Black Bart tried to rob us. Sugar Foot managed to shoot me before I slashed him with my whip, but the bullet went right through my arm. That bungler is dead. Black Bart took off, but he's got a load of buckshot in his backside. It will be some time before he does any more harm."

After yelling for someone to fetch the new doctor in town, Sheriff Egan asked, "Anyone else hurt?"

"Yes, the Widow Teakins" Charlie answered. "That rat bag Black Bart hit her up side her head with his pistol. She took a nasty blow, but I think she'll be fine."

Just then the stagecoach door opened. After Amy and Mr. Olson helped Miss Teakins down, a woman immediately rushed to her side. Not only was she also dressed in black, the woman could have been her twin.

"Sister, I've been so worried," the woman said, taking the widow by her arm and leading her to a horse-drawn buggy. "I must tend to your injury."

"I'll be fine. Charlie dealt with those scoundrels once and for all. They won't be doing any more harm. Mr. Olson has been very kind, and those children were brave. I was wrong about them," she added, giving us a weak smile. As she glanced over at Bo Jangles, the last thing I heard her say to her sister as she led her away was, "I think we should get a critter. A cat will do."

I was speechless. "Goes to show, even when a person seems mean, they might have a good side if you just know where to look," I thought as I watched the horse and buggy head down the road.

The doctor cleaned Charlie's wound and applied a new bandage. You're a lucky man, Charlie," he said. "All you'll have to show for that near miss will be a scar. You did it again. You got the mail and money box through safely."

Turning to Presley, Amy, and me, the sheriff said, "Got a telegram about you kids. Heard you are looking for a parent, but you don't remember much else."

"We're looking for my mother," I said. "All we remember is falling out of a tree." Presley and Amy nodded their heads in agreement.

"What tree?" the sheriff asked with a confused look on his face.

"The one in the courtyard at the Stagecoach Inn in Salado."

For a minute, the sheriff was quiet as he looked at us intently. "I don't like lies, but Widow Teakins says you are good young 'uns. Coming from her, that's something. Charlie agrees with her. Over the years, he's proven to be a good judge of character. Miss Elizabeth, the teacher in Salado, is well respected. She believes all of you have suffered some sort of shock that has caused you to lose your memories, so I'll leave things be for the time being."

"Tell me about your mother," the sheriff said, turning to me.

"The night before she disappeared, we had a fight, and I told her I hated her," I said, struggling not to cry as my mind turned back to that painful memory. "The next morning, I wanted to tell her I was sorry, but she was gone. I've been looking for her ever since."

"Hmm. How old is she and what does she look like?"

"She's thirty-five, and she's beautiful. She has long red hair, and everyone loves her."

"Where's your father?"

"He was in the war. That's all I remember." The problem with lying is when you tell one, you're forced to follow it with another. Again, I crossed my fingers behind my back.

"And you, young man?"

"I used to live at the Stagecoach Inn at a different time, but it's not the same."

"If you're an escaped slave, you don't need to be afraid," the sheriff said, turning to Amy. "Lincoln won the war, and slavery was abolished."

"I'm not a slave. I came here to help Sophie find her mother. She's my best friend."

"Where are you from?"

"Sudan."

"Where on earth is that?"

"Africa."

Looking baffled, the sheriff said. "This is all beyond me. Sophie, if I find your mother, I'll wire the sheriff in Salado immediately."

That evening, we were invited for dinner at the sheriff's home. As soon as we arrived, Amy went to the kitchen where Mrs. Egan was preparing a meal. While we sat in the parlor, Charlie proceeded to tell the sheriff how Sugar Foot and Black Bart tried to rob the stage. When he got to the part about Bingo attacking Sugar Foot and Bo Jangles jumping on Black Bart's neck, the sheriff looked down at Bingo in disbelief. Sprawled on his back and lying next to my feet with his tongue hanging out, Bingo looked anything but dangerous. Instead, he looked downright silly.

"You're joshin' me. That's no attack dog. He's the strangest looking little mutt I've ever seen. By the size of him, he'd barely make an appetizer for a coyote."

"You'd be surprised," Charlie said with a grin. "He may be little, but in his doggie mind, I suspect he sees himself as one of those huge Chinese mastiff guard dogs I've read about. Wish you could have seen him latched onto Sugar Foot's leg. That gib face was doing a frantic dance trying to shake him off."

Shaking his head in disbelief, the sheriff then looked at Bo Jangles who was draped across my lap. You could hear him purring clear across the room. "Next thing you'll tell me is that the cat on Sophie's lap thinks it's a mountain lion."

"Could be," Charlie laughed. "I've never seen a bandit look so panicked as Black Bart when that cat landed on his neck."

Just before dinner was served, Amy took me aside. "Mrs. Egan only has a wood-burning stove. I saw her put her hand in the open oven to gauge the temperature, and she knew exactly when it was right. While bread was baking, she had several dishes cooking on top. She even has to get water from a hand pump. I don't know how she does it."

When we sat down at the table, covered with a crocheted lace tablecloth, and set with china and silver, we were served a meal that was fit for a king. Savoring each bite, I thought about the restaurants that mom and dad used to take me to when Dad was home on leave. As far as I was concerned, this food was as good, if not better, than the food served in those expensive eateries, and it was all prepared without the benefits of electric appliances and microwaves. While we ate, the sheriff proceeded to tell us about the events that happened right before we arrived.

"I got a telegram a few weeks ago that Sam Bass and his gang robbed the Union Pacific train up East. They got away with $60,000 in newly minted fifty-dollar gold pieces, along with silver bullion. They also robbed the passengers, taking $1,300 worth of gold watches and rings. Most of the gang got caught, but Sam disguised himself as a farmer and got away. When he made it back to Texas, he formed his own gang, but one of the gang betrayed him and got word to the Texas Rangers that he was headed our way."

With a sad expression, he continued, "Hard to believe that at one time Sam was my friend. Never thought he'd become an outlaw. We weren't sure when he would arrive. When Deputy Grimes saw a man lounging in front of the bank, he got suspicious thinking it might be a stakeout by the gang. He approached the man and asked if he was armed. It was Sam Bass. Pretending to hand over his gun, Bass shot Grimes dead. It was flat out murder. Major Jones, a Texas Ranger, was in the barbershop getting a shave. When he heard the shot, he ran out into the street, still lathered up. He shot Bass in the head, wounding him mortally. He was found a short time later in a field and died right after they brought him to town."

"Isn't that a good thing?" Presley asked. "Those men with you when we arrived didn't look happy."

"Because of Sam's notoriety, people are afraid that when word gets out, a lot of bandits will head this way."

"What happened to the gold and silver?" I asked.

"Bass never told anyone. Rumor has it that he hid it in this part of Texas."

That night Presley, Amy, and I shared a bedroom in the sheriff's house. Charlie insisted on sleeping in the stable with the horses. As usual, Bingo was sleeping at Presley's feet, and Bo Jangles was purring with his head on my cheek.

As the cool night breeze ruffled the lace curtains in the open window, I thought about the gold. "I wonder if it will ever be found," I wondered before drifting off to asleep.

Chapter 7

Upon our return to Salado, word already had spread about the attempted robbery during our trip to Round Rock. Charlie was unerringly polite as people congratulated him on his bravery, but I could tell those compliments made him uncomfortable. There was little sympathy about Sugar Foot's death. Some even found it amusing that Charlie had filled Black Bart's rear end with buckshot.

Kate seemed particularly interested in what had happened to Sam Bass.

"I'm pretty sure he was a guest at the hotel a few weeks ago," she said. "He used a different name when he checked in, but I'm sure it was him. He was a spiffy dresser. You'd never take him for a robber or a cold-blooded murderer. He was with two brothers, Jesse and Frank James. Jesse was the flamboyant one. He took a hankering to Cora Belle, one of my girls. She said he had a lot of fifty-dollar gold pieces and didn't hesitate to spend them. While his brother Frank sat in the lobby reading a book, Jesse went to Cora Belle's room. She said later all he could talk about was how much he hated Union soldiers."

As I listened to Kate's account, I tried to keep a neutral expression on my face. Glancing at Presley and Amy, I realized they were doing the same. Kate had no way of knowing much about those men, but the three of us were from the future. We not only knew some of their history, we knew the outcome. I decided I wanted to hear more.

"This is interesting," I said casually. "What else did Jesse tell Cora Belle?"

"Jesse told Cora Belle the Union militia had raided their farm looking for Frank and his gang when Jesse was just a boy. They tortured his stepfather and hanged him from a tree. Even though Jesse was just a kid, they lashed him. When he was seventeen, he joined Quantrill's Confederate guerrillas. When he tried to surrender under a flag of truce, a Union soldier shot him in the stomach, almost killing him."

As Kate talked, I couldn't tell her that Jesse and Frank James would commit so many train and bank robberies throughout the West they would become legends. Their stories would be told in movies and novels popular even in the 21st century.

I grew thoughtful as I thought about what the James brothers went through before they became outlaws. I began to understand their crimes were not just about greed; they were motivated by rage. I thought back to one of my mother's sayings, "Hatred is like drinking poison and waiting for the other person to die."

"When did they leave?" I asked.

"The next day. The three of them were acting strange the night before. They kept going in and out of the hotel all night long. I could hear them talking in low voices. When I walked by, they grew silent. I'm glad they're gone."

Knowing how dangerous these men were, I didn't blame Kate for being relieved when the three outlaws left, but I couldn't help but wonder what they were doing here in the first place.

As the story about our exploits spread, people loved hearing about the actions of Bo Jangles and Bingo. Sometimes we could hear people laughing and talking about them on the boardwalk outside the hotel. "You two are becoming household names," I told my pets one day. "I just hope it doesn't go to your heads." The response was an enthusiastic tail wag from Bingo. With an inscrutable expression on his face, Bo Jangles simply licked his paws.

One afternoon, a little girl came into the lobby and approached me. Gazing at Bo Jangles, who was on my lap, and Bingo, who was at Presley's feet, she asked, "Are these them? The pets who saved the day when those bandits tried to rob the coach?"

I was surprised that Charlie's heroism wasn't being mentioned, but I nodded my head.

"Can I pet them?"

"Of course. Don't worry. They won't bite you."

She knelt and began stroking Bo Jangles. His purr increased in volume. Then, she sat down next to Bingo who, happy for the attention, immediately rolled over on his back so she could scratch his belly. With his tongue hanging out, the look on his face was one of pure bliss.

To my surprise, she took two small, colorful scarves out of her purse and tied them around Bingo and Bo Jangles' necks. Bo Jangles' scarf was blue, and she had embroidered his name in yellow. Bingo's scarf was red, and his name was embroidered in black. Bo Jangles licked her hand, and Bingo gave her a sloppy kiss.

"These two think this attention is their due," I told Amy after the girl left. "In their minds, they're the real heroes in this story."

From that time on, there was no need to slip tidbits of food under the table when we ate. Hayley served Bo Jangles a bowl of milk, and if there happened to be fish on the menu, that was an extra treat. Bingo sometimes got a serving of steak. "If we ever make it back to the 21st century, these two are in for a shock," I told Presley. "They might have a hard time settling for regular dog and cat food."

As one day faded into the next, even though I found this period and the people who lived in it fascinating, at times I was bored. I think Amy and Presley felt the same way. To make matters worse, I couldn't stop thinking about my mother. "Where are you?" I implored silently, trying to recall her beautiful face, even though it was getting harder and harder to remember what she looked like.

One day, Miss Elizabeth asked us to meet her in the lobby. "Children, I have an idea," she said when we arrived. "I don't think it's good for young people your age to be stuck in this hotel, and I know, even when you're walking around outside, there's not much to see. I've asked Hayley to fix a picnic basket, and I want all of you to explore. There's much to be learned from nature."

"That's a wonderful idea," Presley said. Both Amy and I agreed wholeheartedly.

"Just be back before supper, Presley. I've talked to Kate, and she wants you to play the piano this evening. More and more people are coming to hear you play. The restaurant is fully booked for the entire week." Taking me by the hand, Miss Elizabeth led me to a corner.

"Have you remembered anything yet, dear?"

"All I remember is that at one time, we were in a very strange land. I'm beginning to suspect I won't find my mother," I said, fighting tears.

"Don't fret, dear," she said, patting my arm. "I know your mother and father would both be very proud of you."

Another lie. After she walked away, I felt ashamed. I hated lying and deceiving people, especially Miss Elizabeth. "There's no other way," I told myself. "No one would believe us."

The next morning Tom and Isadora were waiting for us in the lobby. Presley carried the picnic basket as we made our way out to the front steps. To our surprise, Charlie came around the corner leading two horses. "These two girls are gentle," he said. "Presley, you and Tom can ride double. The girls are lightweights, so the three of them can all ride together."

Minutes later we headed out of town. I hadn't realized how beautiful the terrain in South Texas was. Unspoiled by telephone wires and speeding cars on a busy interstate, the rolling hills, ponds with surfaces that glistened like glass, and groves of trees reminded me of photos in one of the coffee-table books so popular in the modern world. A few hours later, we spread out the picnic underneath a large shade tree. There was sweet tea in a jug, sandwiches, pickled eggs, and cake. We devoured every bite.

Later, we spotted a magnificent waterfall that spilled into a pond. A Snowy White Egret stood fishing at the edge. Watching him for a few minutes, it was obvious he would never go hungry.

While Bingo chased squirrels without success, Bo Jangles honed his hunting skills by stalking anything that moved in the grass. When he finally caught a lizard and presented it to me as a gift, I had to laugh at the look of disappointment and surprise on his face when I let it go.

I had never seen so many birds. Perched in trees, they seemed unafraid as we approached.

"So many of these birds are so colorful," I said. "I've never seen some of them before."

"Aunt Elizabeth loves birds," Tom said. "She says the reason there are so many birds here is because of the mild climate."

"What are some of their names?" Presley asked.

"There are red cardinals, green jays, ringed kingfishers, grey hawks, and lots of hummingbirds just to name a few. There's too many for me to remember."

We climbed rock cliffs, and when we finally got tired, we lay in the grass and stared at fluffy clouds floating in a sky that was an incredible shade of blue. "What shape do you see in that big cloud directly above us?" I asked Isadora.

"An elephant," was the immediate response.

I managed not to laugh, knowing the only elephant she had ever seen was a picture in a book.

"Aunt Elizabeth told us we need to pick some flowers," she said. "She wants us to press them in a book along with their names so we can share them with the other students when we start school."

There was an amazing array of flowers. "Not anything like prehistoric Texas," I noted to myself, "but beautiful just the same."

The variety of plants was almost too numerous to count. They included what is known as the chili Pequin (a spicy, orange-red edible fruit), sprawling trumpet vines that seemed to cover anything and everything, Jack in the Bush covered with small blue flowers, yarrow, a variety of lilies, red carnations, Indian paintbrush, Mexican heather, lantana, Rock rose, firebush, oxeye daisies, columbine, and pink sage.

It wasn't long before Tom and Presley lost interest in picking flowers.

"We're going to go up the hill to see if we can spot some deer," Presley announced.

"Or a bear, or maybe even a mountain lion," Tom said hopefully.

Seeing the look of alarm on Amy's face, I laughed. "Don't forget coyotes, wolves, and bobcats."

"Do you think wild animals might attack us?" Amy asked, looking worried. "Some of our people got attacked by lions in Africa when they were trying to get to refugee camps."

"My dad used to say most animals are afraid of humans. If we leave them alone, more than likely, they'll leave us alone. Don't worry. We're perfectly safe."

When we mounted our horses and headed back to Salado, the sky was splashed with amazing colors of reds, golds, and violets in a sunset that was so breathtaking it hardly seemed real.

"Presley, I wish this day could have gone on forever," I said.

"You're not alone," he replied, "even if we didn't rustle up a bear or mountain lion."

Isadora had fallen asleep and was slumped against me, and Amy, sitting behind me with her arms around my waist, had her cheek resting on my shoulder. Then, without warning, my mood did a complete shift. Suddenly, I was so frightened the hair on the back of my neck stood up. Instinct told me that in the following days, something would happen that would terrify us. As I looked over at Presley, his face, usually animated, was relaxed and peaceful. Tom looked proud and happy. His feelings toward Presley bordered on hero worship, and I sensed much of his happiness stemmed from the fact he had spent an entire day with his idol. Determined not to spoil the mood, I decided not to say a word. I just knew we would face danger, but I had no idea what it would be.

Chapter 8

When we arrived back at the hotel, I was surprised to see a man, dressed all in black, standing on the steps. More than likely, I wouldn't have paid attention to him except for the fact he was surrounded by a group of men. Tall and thin, he wore what is called a frock coat and appeared to be preaching a sermon. I noticed a young Native American man leaning against the wall watching him a short distance away. Motionless, his dark eyes remained fixed on the speaker.

"Are you saved?" the man in black yelled. Before anyone could answer, he continued. "If you don't go to church, you're not saved. If you drink or smoke, you're not saved. That means you're going to hell, as you well should."

"We don't kill people. Does that count?" a voice asked from the crowd.

"Who said that?"

There was no answer. Instead, I could see some of the people looking at the ground. Others were gazing around as if hoping for an escape.

"Why don't they leave?" I wondered. They were afraid.

When we got off our horses and started up the steps, I got a closer look. A shiver went down my back when I saw the man's eyes. Cold and black, they were flat and without expression. His lips, pressed in a sharp line, outlined a mouth that I was sure never smiled.

Catching sight of us, he yelled, pointing at me, Amy, and Presley. "Are you the ones that everyone's talking about? See that black heathen? She dares to walk among us! No one seems to know where you came from," he yelled as he turned to me and Presley. "I know where you came from and who you are. You came from hell, and you're the devil's spawn, here to corrupt this town and bring damnation upon these pathetic souls."

Stunned, Presley, Amy, and I just stood there. Tom looked frightened but said bravely, "You can't talk that way about my friends, Mister. They're good, and everybody knows it."

"The devil is a liar and the great deceiver. They've fooled you, and they've fooled everyone around here. But they don't fool me. I'm God's Angel of Justice, and I will stop them!"

Isadora started to cry. Presley moved in front of Tom, and I pushed Isadora behind me. I didn't know who this man was, but I knew without a doubt, he was not only a fanatic, he was dangerous. Before we could respond, the front door opened. Miss Elizabeth and Kate rushed out, and, without a glance or a word in the man's direction, herded us into the hotel.

Looking back, I saw the sheriff approaching. I was surprised to see he looked apprehensive.

"Who is that crazy man?" Presley asked once we were inside.

"He's James Brown Miller. Some call him Deacon Jim because he goes to church every Sunday and fancies himself a preacher. Others call him Killer Miller."

"He's religious, but he kills people?" I asked, confused.

"He murdered his own grandparents when he was eight years old. When he was grown, he had an argument with his brother-in-law. Waiting until he was asleep, he killed him, too. He's killed several people over the years."

"Why isn't he in prison?" Presley asked.

"He's smart and always manages to get off – either with a technicality or by bribing the jury. At one point, he was with the Texas Rangers. For a while, he was the deputy sheriff in Pecos where he took great delight in killing Mexicans. Now, he gets paid to kill people. He's an assassin."

"In the modern world, we'd call him a serial killer," I thought.

Just then, shots rang out. Rushing out the door, we found the sheriff lying in the dirt. Charlie was slumped over a few feet away. Miller was nowhere to be seen. The Native American also had vanished. The crowd, who had been listening to Miller minutes earlier, had scattered. They emerged slowly from their hiding places and gathered around us.

"Get Dr. Barton," Kate screamed as she lifted the sheriff's head and put it in her lap. Blood was seeping out of his chest, and his eyes were closed. Minutes later, Dr. Welborn Barton, accompanied by his wife Adeline and two hired hands, pulled up in their buggy. While the sheriff was being carried to the doctor's buggy, Kate turned her attention to Charlie. "Charlie will be fine," she said. "He suffered a blow to the head, but he's unhurt."

Once he was able to sit up, Charlie said, "I shot Miller right after he shot the sheriff. Got him in the chest. When I opened his coat, that black villain had a metal plate strapped to his chest. I looked up just in time to see the Indian hit me on the head with the butt of a pistol. That's the last thing I remember."

"I think you got hit by that Indian who goes by the name Apache Kid," Kate said. "You are lucky he didn't kill you. He's so evil he's been banished by his own tribe."

"What did he do?" I asked.

"For one thing, he captured an Apache woman. When he got tired of her, he killed her and captured another. He's what is known as a 'lone wolf.' He's been arrested several times but always manages to escape."

"Why do you think he was here?" I asked Kate.

"I suspect he started out following Killer Miller, but obviously, he's decided to join him. With those two working together, things are more dangerous than ever."

Later that evening, I thought back to the premonition I had during my ride back to Salado. As I replayed the events in my mind, I knew that the run-in with Killer Miller was just the beginning. Even though he made it clear he hated us on sight, despite everything that happened, we weren't hurt. "There's more to come," I decided. "We'll be lucky to survive."

Chapter 9

After a few days, when it became obvious the man described as Killer Miller and Deacon Jim, would not return, people seemed relieved. I had hoped things would go back to normal, but they didn't. Apparently, his remarks about us had made an impression on some of the citizens. Now when we went outside, not everyone we ran into seemed happy to see us. When they did see us, they looked frightened. Even though they were polite, they looked at us strangely, as if they were trying to figure out if we were good or bad. Because they didn't know who we were or where we came from, Miller's accusations had caused people to become suspicious. Presley and I could not explain we were from the future. Revealing where we came from would not be believed and, more than likely, would add fire to that awful man's rant. One day, when we were walking along the boardwalk, a woman, holding a child's hand, took one look at us and hurried across the street.

"I can't believe this," I said that evening to Miss Elizabeth and Hayley after telling them about the incident. "How can anyone believe that horrible man?"

"I am so sorry, dear," Miss Elizabeth said. "A lot of the people here have little or no education. They fear the unknown. There is a lot of poverty since the war ended. Entire plantations, along with small farms, were burned down. Livestock was taken, crops were ruined, and property and food was stolen. It's often the case that when people feel they're being punished by God, they look for a scapegoat. When a man like Deacon Jim comes along, he plays on people's insecurities and fears. No matter what he does, or how bad he is, if he claims to be a man of God, some people believe him. Miller is a man who does not bring people together. He divides them."

"Some people act like sheep," Hayley sniffed. "They'll let others tell them what to think even when the facts are as clear as day."

"We don't care what people say about you. We are your friends," Tom said.

"Yes, best friends. I hate that mean old man that said terrible things about you," Isadora added, stamping her foot.

Too touched to speak, I crossed the room and gave her a hug. Presley shook Tom's hand. "We're lucky to have friends like you," he said.

"Yes, we are," Amy added.

As if he had been following the entire conversation, Bingo barked. Bo Jangles jumped off the bed, purred loudly, and slowly wound his graceful feline form around Isadora's ankles.

We all laughed. "Well, that settles it. The vote is unanimous," I announced.

That night I thought long and hard about what Miss Elizabeth had said. "Do you think a lot of the people we see in town are poor?" I asked Presley.

"Yes. Some even look like they're hungry."

"Even though black people are free, a lot of them don't have enough to eat," Amy said, "I have talked to some of them. Many of them are going North to look for jobs."

The next day, as we walked around trying not to be too obvious, I looked at people's faces. I noticed that many of the children were pale and thin. When I looked closely at some of the people's garments, I noticed their clothes were threadbare. "I can't believe I'm just now realizing this," I thought.

That evening at dinner, I asked Kate to join us. "I didn't realize how terrible things were," I said. "I feel bad that I never even noticed."

"It's hard to understand, or even recognize something you've never experienced. I don't know where you're from, but I know you've never been poor."

"How can you tell?" Presley asked.

"Because you have a musical gift, you had to have had an instrument to play on. And talent must be guided, so my guess is you've had training. Most people here have never owned a piano. Also, you and Sophie both exude self-confidence. That does not go hand in hand with poverty."

Looking at Amy, she added, "I believe that when it comes to poverty, of the three of you, you've probably come the closest."

"Why do you say that?" Amy asked.

"You said you're from Africa. From what I've heard, there's a lot of poverty in that world. Also, you're very thin."

"Almost all of the Sudanese are thin," Amy replied. "That's just the way we are, but yes, we had a hard time before my mother came to this country. We lived in a refugee camp where we only got one meal a day. When we came to America, we couldn't even speak English."

I stayed silent. Even though at one time I had thought of myself as skinny, I wasn't anymore. Looking in the mirror earlier that day, I had been pleased to see that my skin looked rosy, and my hair was shiny. I was the picture of health.

Reaching over and taking my hand, Miss Kate said, "No matter. I know in my heart all of you children have good hearts. Don't let that evil man who calls himself a man of God affect you. He has absolutely no conscience. If anyone's the devil's spawn, it's him."

Having just entered the room, Haley had overheard part of our conversation. "Anyone with any sense realizes what kind of people you are," she said. "The others don't count. Don't let them upset you."

That night, lying on the pallet on the floor, I found it difficult to sleep. My mind seemed to spin from one thought to another, going back again and again to the news that Black Bart had stolen $60,000 worth of fifty-dollar gold coins and silver bullion. I wondered if there was any truth to the rumor that the gold and silver was hidden some place in this area.

"We could do so much with that money if we could find it," I thought. "We'd help everybody in Salado. We'd buy food and clothing and have a huge party."

Suddenly, I got excited. "If anyone can find it, it's us," I decided. Going to the window, I peered out into the night. The full moon magnified everything, illuminating in stark detail the buildings and trees. It was then I noticed a man leaning against a building. It was the young Native American. Even at a distance, I could have sworn he was glaring at me with a look of complete hatred. Startled, I hurried back to my pallet and lay down. "I wonder why he was staring at me," I pondered. Moments later, I had forgotten all about him as I fantasized about what we would do once we were rich. "We need to find that gold," was my last thought before going to sleep.

Chapter 10

The next morning, I woke up feeling excited and refreshed. Tom and Isadora, along with Presley and Amy, were already in the dining room. As usual, Hayley, who was helping serve breakfast, was giving us extra portions before placing Bingo's and Bo Jangle's dishes on the floor.

"After you're finished eating, I want to talk to all of you," I said before sitting down at the table.

"What's going on?" Tom asked.

"Nothing serious. I want to play a game when we're finished."

"What game?" Presley asked.

"We're going on a treasure hunt."

"A treasure hunt?" they all said in unison.

"I love treasures," Isadora said happily.

"After breakfast, let's meet outside and then go to the stable. Maybe Charlie can help us."

There was little conversation as everyone hastily finished their breakfast. My remarks about a treasure hunt had piqued everyone's interest.

"There's so much poverty here," I said once we got outside the hotel. "Many of the children look like they're hungry. I think we should try to help."

"How?" Presley asked.

"Do you remember when the sheriff in Round Rock said Sam Bass robbed a train and hid the huge amount of gold and silver he got in the robbery?"

"Yes," Presley said.

"He refused to tell anyone where it was before he died. Some people think he hid it in this area. Can you imagine how much that money could help these people?"

"Why do you think it's here?" Amy asked.

"Miss Kate thinks he, along with Frank and Jesse James, used aliases and stayed in the hotel shortly after the robbery. She told me they were acting strangely the day before they left. She mentioned they were going in and out of the hotel all night long. Also, they were very secretive."

"I see where this is going," Presley said.

"What about our treasure hunt?" Isadora asked, looking disappointed.

"The stolen gold and silver are the treasure," I pointed out. "If we all work together, I think we can find it. When we do, we can help a lot of people."

"True," Amy added. "A lot of the black people I know won't have to go North."

"I like to help people," Isadora said seriously.

"Me, too," Tom said. "Aunt Elizabeth says when we help others, we help ourselves."

Without another word, we headed for the stables. When we arrived, Charlie was rubbing down one of his horses. When I told him I thought the shipment of gold and silver that Sam Bass stole could be hidden on the hotel grounds, he looked at us thoughtfully.

"Could be," he said. "I remember the day he and the James brothers arrived. I didn't realize who they were at the time. I noticed they were struggling to carry several heavy sacks. When I offered to help, they refused even though I could tell the bags were very heavy. I think they carried them up into their rooms. Later, they kept walking around as if they were looking for something. The three of them would take off in different directions. Then, they'd return and minutes later start the same routine all over again."

"Do you know what they did with the sacks?" Presley asked.

"Nope. I had to run errands for Miss Kate. When I got back, they had left. I assumed they took the sacks with them."

Now I was even more excited. "Do you think they might be hidden somewhere near here?"

"We're going to find the treasure," Isadora said, jumping up and down with excitement. "Then we can help people."

"There are a lot of places to look," Charlie said doubtfully. "It will be like looking for a needle in a haystack."

"You're right," Presley said. "This place is huge. If they hid it here, it could be any place."

"I've got something that might help." Without another word, Charlie went to the tack room. When he came back, he had a large paper scroll in his hand.

"Is that a map?" Tom asked, his eyes shining with excitement.

"It's that and more," Charlie said as he unrolled the scroll on top of stacked bundles of hay. We gathered around staring down at the unfurled document. Looking at the faded ink marks, I could see drawings of buildings along with illustrations of trees, roads, and creeks.

"This is not only a map; it's a detailed plot diagram that was used when the hotel was built," Charlie explained. "As you can see, it shows in detail all the buildings and drawings and details of the surrounding natural terrain. This should make your treasure hunt easier."

"Let's start right now," Presley said as Charlie handed him the scroll.

"Be careful," Charlie warned. "This is not only a big area to cover, but there are abandoned sheds, old wells, and caves."

"We need a plan," Presley said. "We can't just run around all over the place."

"What do you have in mind?" Tom asked.

"We'll start at the outer perimeter and work our way in. Does anyone have any string? Also, it would help to have some paint." Presley advised.

"I've got just the thing," Tom said before rushing back to the hotel.

"Me, too," Isadora added as she ran after him.

They quickly returned. Tom had a ball of string in his hands, and Isadora was carrying her metal box filled with paints. I knew how much she treasured them. "Are you sure you want to use your paints?" I asked. "This could require quite a lot."

"Yes," she replied solemnly. "I want to help people."

Starting at one edge of the property, we moved slowly, covering every inch of ground. Once we were finished, we chose Isadora's favorite color, yellow, and dabbed it on the trees in the area we had covered. We tied the string around areas filled with brush once we had searched them.

Apparently, Bo Jangles and Bingo knew exactly what was going on and decided to help. Bingo, deadly serious with his nose to the ground, moved ahead of us. No longer in his silly-dog mode, he seemed as intent on finding the treasure as we were. As for Bo Jangles, he, too, was trying to help. Once we marked a tree with paint, he moved to the next one, looking back at us expectantly.

"Be careful when you open any doors to these old shacks. You never know what might be in them," Amy warned.

"Yes, like snakes. Some of these sheds haven't been used for years," Tom said.

"Ugh. Probably spiders too," Amy added.

I didn't tell the others, but I had a feeling we were being watched. Moving slowly, I would stop, turn, and listen, but I could never see anything suspicious. "Just my imagination," I told myself, shaking off my apprehension.

The others spread out and were soon out of sight. I could hear the distant sounds of old, warped doors being yanked open along with the screeching protest of rusty iron fittings that hadn't been opened in years.

Coming to a shed, I saw that one of the glass panes in the window was broken. Peering into it, I didn't see anything at first. As I turned away to open the door, out of the corner of my eye, I saw movement. Looking in again, I saw a large skunk and her three babies. Jumping back from the window, I knew this was one shed I would not enter. Years earlier, my mom had told me about her experience with skunks when she was a little girl visiting her friend's farm. "Skunks aren't afraid of anything because they have a secret weapon, which I discovered the hard way," she had said. "I happened to stumble onto a mother skunk and her kittens. I decided the kittens were too small to spray me, so I picked one up. Not only did it spray me, it bit my thumb. After that, I had to spend hours in the bathtub filled with water laced with vinegar, canned tomatoes, and bleach. When I got out, I used a whole bottle of Evening in Paris perfume to get rid of the smell. Even then, it lingered for a few days."

As I turned away, Isadora, accompanied by Bingo and Bo Jangles, rounded the corner.

"Don't go in there, Isadora," I warned. "There's a skunk inside."

Even before I got the words out of my mouth, Bingo was backing up with his tail tucked between his legs, and Bo Jangles darted up a tree. Animals and humans alike, we beat a hasty retreat.

Moving on to the next shed, I cautiously opened the door. Seeing nothing more frightening than a huge spider web, I closed the door after looking around and continued my search. Even though we searched for hours, we didn't find anything out of the ordinary.

"I didn't know a treasure hunt could take so long," Isadora said wearily. Impressed by the fact that never once did she wander off to play, I gave her a quick hug.

"What makes a treasure a treasure?" I asked.

"I don't know, Sophie."

"Because treasures aren't everyday things, they are rarely in plain sight. Usually, they're hard to find. The harder they are to find, the more important they are. That's what makes them a treasure."

Thinking for a minute, Isadora nodded her head. "Now I understand why treasures are treasures, Sophie." With that, she headed toward a pile of rocks.

Looking at her as she continued searching, my heart ached. "If we ever find my mother and get back to our world, I'll be happy," I thought, "but in some ways, it will break my heart. Losing Isadora will be like losing the best little sister in the world."

As I rounded a corner and headed toward a grove of trees, I was startled to see someone dart behind a pile of boulders. I was sure it was the same Native American I had seen with Deacon Jim. Standing still, I yelled, "Come out! Why are you following us?"

There was no answer. Instead, everything was quiet. The silence seemed so heavy I could feel it pressing down on my shoulders. Even the birds were silent. Feeling uneasy, I continued to stand in the same spot for a few minutes. Finally, I headed toward the others.

Late that afternoon, we went back to the hotel. Exhausted, Isadora, Tom, and Amy went to our room. Presley and I sat on the veranda.

"Do you still think we'll find it?" Presley asked.

"We have to. We haven't searched everything. It has to be here somewhere."

Presley opened the map and spread it out in front of us. "Maybe we missed something," After we stared at it for several minutes, he started to roll it back up. "I don't think we've missed anything."

"Wait!" I almost shouted. "I think I saw something!"

Looking at me in surprise, he unrolled the map again. Peering down, I stared at the drawing of the hotel. "Look," I said as I pointed to the side of the building. I slowly moved my finger to a huge mound that seemed to have been piled directly against the wall. Looking closely, I could barely make out what seemed to be the outline of a wooden door. Covered in vines and branches, it was almost completely hidden. The faded words next to an arrow pointed directly at the door read, "Entrance to the Cave."

Chapter 11

The next morning, Miss Elizabeth sat down beside us while we were eating. "Tom and Isadora, we will be spending the day going over your lessons. School will start soon, and you need to be ready."

"But we're looking for treasure," Isadora protested.

"I'm sorry, dear, the treasure will have to wait. You can look for it later."

"Could we do it tomorrow?" Tom asked hopefully. "We promised Sophie, Presley, and Amy we'd help them."

"No," was the firm reply. "This is about priorities." Smiling at us she said, "I know your friends will understand."

Minutes later, we watched as Aunt Elizabeth walked up the stairs, followed by a reluctant Tom and Isadora.

Silent for a minute, the three of us looked at each other.

"I know Tom and Isadora are disappointed, but I think it's for the best," Presley said.

"I do, too," Amy added. "Isadora got very tired yesterday."

"Sometimes things happen for a reason," I said. "When Presley and I looked at the map again last night, I saw something I hadn't noticed before," I explained, turning to Amy. "It was a huge clue. If I'm right, I don't know if it would be safe to take Isadora and Tom with us."

"A clue? What is it?" Amy asked, her eyes wide with excitement.

"The map shows a large mound of earth next to the wall of the hotel, The ink on the map is so faded, it's hard to make everything out, but I think I saw the outline of a door. An arrow in red ink was pointed to it with the words 'Entrance to the Cave.'"

Without another word, the three of us jumped up, ran outside, and raced around to the side of the building. When we saw the ground was perfectly flat, we ran to the other side. Not visible from the road, it would be unusual for anyone to walk past this area unless they had a specific reason. To our delight, there was a large mound covered with grass and weeds. At first, we almost walked past the wooden door. It had been painted at one time, but time and neglect had faded the color until it was barely visible. With tree roots and vines hanging over the exterior, it was almost completely hidden. Looking closely, we could see someone recently had dug into the packed earth at the bottom of the door and had opened it. Before whomever it was had left, they had piled dirt and rocks halfway up the door's exterior to make sure no one else could enter.

"Someone's been here before us," Presley said. "If there is nothing in there, why would they care if anyone wanted to open this door?"

Discouraged, I looked at the pile of rubble. "They've gone to a lot of trouble to make sure no one else can get in. I don't know if we can get the door open."

"We've come this far, and we're not giving up now," Presley replied. With that, he began pulling tree roots and branches away from the top of the door. Amy disappeared and returned in a few minutes, carrying an old shovel and pickax. "I knew we'd find something useful in one of those sheds," she announced.

"What? No snakes or spiders?" I laughed.

"It doesn't matter," Amy replied. "We're going to get that door open, come hell or high water."

"Has anyone seen Bingo or Bo Jangles?" I asked. "I haven't seen them all day."

"They're probably off exploring," Presley said.

We started to dig and move the rocks. Some of them were huge. Presley would swing the pickax, loosening clumps of dirt. Using the shovel, Amy and I took turns pushing the dirt out of the way. At one point, we even used our hands. It took a long time to dig back down to the bottom of the door. Finally, using all our strength, we were able to pull the door partially open. Looking inside, we were excited to see a tunnel. By this time, it was getting dark.

"Do you think we should wait until tomorrow?" Amy asked.

"No. I don't want anyone to see us. If we happen to find anything and others find out, it could cause a stampede."

"Wait here. I'll be right back," Presley said before racing to the stable. He quickly returned with a lantern. "I told Charlie what we've found," he said. "He warned us to be careful."

"I'm surprised he didn't come with you," I said.

"He wanted to, but one of his horses is sick. He said if we waited until tomorrow, he would join us. I told him what you said about not letting others know about our search for the treasure. He agrees."

As we walked through the tunnel behind the door, it gradually widened and sloped downward. After several minutes, we turned a corner and found ourselves in a large cave. The high ceilings were covered in stalactites, some reaching almost to the floor.

"Can you believe this is directly under the hotel?" Presley said.

"No one would ever guess," Amy said. "This cave has probably been here for hundreds of years."

"Probably millions of years," I said, thinking back to the cave Presley and I had explored when we were trapped in prehistoric Texas.

When Presley held up the lantern, we saw a chair next to a wooden crate that had obviously been used as a table. A candle, burnt down to a stub, was next to a rusty tin cup. Spotting a tarp covering something in the corner, I grabbed an end and pulled it off. Several bags, piled one on top of the other, were stacked against the cave wall. One of the bags had tipped over, spilling out the contents. Fifty-dollar gold pieces and silver bars littered the floor.

At first, all we could do was stare. "We found it!" I said, my voice shaking with excitement. "I can't believe it. We actually found it."

"I bet there's enough money here to help the entire town for months to come," Presley said happily.

Our happiness was short lived. Hearing a noise, we turned around.

To my horror, Killer Miller (or Deacon Jim, as some knew him) accompanied by the Apache Kid, stepped out of the shadows.

"You found it alright, but you won't be giving it to anyone," Killer Miller said. His mouth, which I had believed incapable of anything but a frown, was turned upward into an evil grin.

"You've done a good job of following these devil's spawn," Killer Miller said to the Apache Kid. "I told you it would be worthwhile. Now all we need to do is kill them. No one knows where they're from. They don't have any kin around here. We'll leave their bodies here in the cave. They'll never be found. But first," he said, turning to us, "the three of you have work to do. You'll haul these sacks out of the cave."

"You expect us to do your dirty work hauling away this gold and silver, and when we're done, you plan to bring us back here and kill us?" Presley said bravely. "We won't do it, so go ahead and kill us now." Even though Presley's face was white with fear, the look in his eyes was one of defiance.

"Oh, I think you will," said Killer Jim, his black eyes glittering. Walking over to Amy he ran the tip of his pistol down her cheek. "I'll enjoy killing this black savage. If you don't do what I say, I'll start now." Standing motionless, Amy stared into space, a single tear made a path down her face.

"Please don't hurt her," I cried. "We'll help you. Just let us go. We won't tell anyone."

Killer Miller laughed. "I'm going to enjoy this."

Apache Kid grabbed my face with one hand, and with his other hand ran his fingers through my hair. "I'm keeping this one for a time. I'm taking her with me. I like this yellow hair and white skin. She'll make a nice change from the squaws I'm used to." Staring into his eyes, I saw not one glimmer of humanity. "He may have been human at one time, but he's not anymore," I thought. "We don't stand a chance."

As we stood staring in disbelief and shock at these ruthless monsters, Killer Jim traced his knife slowly down Amy's cheek. I watched in horror as droplets of blood seeped out of the shallow cut. "Get moving now," he said pleasantly. "Time is wasting. Work fast, and I might make it easier on you."

Silently, we each grabbed a sack and began dragging them into the tunnel. Holding Presley's lantern, Killer Miller followed with Apache Kid, who was directly behind him.

Minutes later, I heard a noise. Bingo and Bo Jangles came racing through the tunnel toward us. When Bingo latched onto Killer Miller's pant leg, without even looking down, Miller gave him a vicious kick with his spurred boot. With a yelp, Bingo limped to the wall and collapsed. Bo Jangles tried to leap on Apache Kid's neck. The Native American grabbed him in midair, and with one fluid motion, threw him against the tunnel wall. Seeing my pets lying motionless on the ground, I started to weep.

"This is all my fault," I told myself. "We'll all be killed. I'll never find my mother. My father will be heartbroken, and Isadora will be sad. I wish I'd forgotten all about this stupid gold."

Just when I accepted the fact that we were all doomed to die horrible deaths, a small ball of intense light materialized in the air in front of us. Startled, we all stopped. As it floated slowly above me, I could feel intense heat, hotter than anything I could ever have imagined. Gathering speed, it began to expand. The expressions on Killer Miller and Apache Kid's faces were, at first, ones of disbelief, followed by looks of terror. By the time the intense light reached them, it had grown and expanded until it was enormous. The last we saw of Killer Miller before the light enveloped him, he was on his knees. With hands clasped in the air, he was praying to the vengeful god he believed in, a god he thought condoned his murderous actions, but that god would show him no mercy.

As for the Apache Kid, he was spinning in a circle, jabbing his knife at a force he could not see or comprehend. We heard howls and screams, then silence. The light began to shrink and fade until it disappeared. Killer Miller and Apache Kid were gone. There was nothing left but heaps of clothing lying on the floor.

"We need to get out of here," Presley yelled.

Turning back to rescue my pets, I heard an ominous rumble

overhead. "Run," I heard. The word seemed to resonate from a feminine, but unearthly, voice that echoed up and down the tunnel. Undecided, I hesitated. Both Amy and Presley grabbed my arms and began dragging me between them as they ran forward.

"Let me go," I screamed. "I need to get Bingo and Bo Jangles."

"There's no time," Presley yelled. "They're too far back. We have to get out of here. The entire tunnel is beginning to collapse."

As we ran, the tunnel seemed longer than ever. Exhausted, we were staggering and stumbling, finding it harder and harder to keep going. Even though we were a short distance from the entrance of the tunnel, we collapsed. I wanted to get up, but my legs simply wouldn't obey. Choking on dust, I could hear a deafening noise as tons of dirt and rock began falling onto the tunnel floor.

"We'll be buried alive," I wept, covering my face and curling my body into a ball, preparing myself for the worst.

"I've got you. Hang onto this rope." I looked up to see Charlie standing over me. He had tied one end of the rope onto the bridle of his horse, which stood waiting patiently outside the tunnel.

As we grabbed the rope and hung on, Charlie shouted, "Back, Bess. Back."

Wanting desperately to live, I prayed, "God, please save us. I'm sorry for doubting you." I felt a flicker of hope as I heard the obedient horse begin to move slowly backward, pulling the three of us as we hung on for dear life. Just when it seemed we'd never make it, the horse dragged us into the open air. Moments later, there was a thunderous roar that seemed to go on forever from within the tunnel.

Lying on the ground, I turned my head and saw that boulders and dirt had filled the tunnel, blocking it with a wall that no one, or anything, could penetrate.

"I'll never forgive myself for letting you go in there without me," Charlie said. "I'm pretty sure those murdering rat bags have been buried alive in that collapse, a fitting end for them. The world will be a better place without them."

We knew what had happened to Apache Kid and Killer Miller. They were not buried in the rubble. They had been eradicated by a mysterious light. Where it came from, none of us knew, but it had saved our lives. Knowing Charlie would find this hard to believe, we stayed silent.

Again, I started to weep. "I think Bingo and Bo Jangles were buried, too," I wailed. "They were trying to protect us. I've lost the most wonderful pets in the world, and it's all my fault."

Both Presley and Amy put their arms around me as I continued to cry.

"Let's get you out of here," Charlie said. Untying the rope, he began leading his horse back to the stable. Wordlessly, the three of us followed. Still weak, I started to stumble. When Charlie turned back to catch me, he stopped with a stunned look on his face.

"I've never believed in angels, but I do now," he said. Even though he was known for his cool nerve under fire, he was trembling.

As all three of us turned around to see what Charlie was staring at, it was our turn to be stunned. My mother was walking calmly toward us. She was not alone. Bingo was trotting happily beside her, and Bo Jangles, alive and well, was in her arms.

Chapter 12

Seeing me, Bingo raced forward, and when I knelt, he proceeded to cover my face with sloppy kisses. Bo Jangles, purring loudly, jumped onto my shoulder and while making biscuits in my hair with his paws, he rubbed his jaws along my face. Again, I started to cry. This time, my tears were tears of joy.

Mother knelt and put her arms around me.

"I've looked all over for you," I said, wiping the tears out of my eyes.

"I know, darling. I've been here all along."

"I want things to go back to the way they were."

"Nothing remains the same in the physical world. Take you, for instance. You're changing, not only physically but emotionally and mentally as well. And, frankly, I'm pleased by the changes I see. I've changed, too. You don't understand yet, but you will."

Thinking back to our time in prehistoric Texas and remembering how those words at one time upset me, I was surprised that now they didn't. I realized Mom was right. I had changed.

After we stood, I glanced at Charlie. With a stunned look on his face, he stood seemingly rooted to the spot he was in when he first saw my mother. Presley and Amy stood a few feet away. Although Amy still looked a little frightened, Presley just looked relieved.

"You saved us again," he said.

"Come, everyone," Mother said. "I think we should get as far as possible from this scene so we can start forgetting about the negative experience that almost took your lives. Please join us," she said, nodding to Charlie. "You are the only one I trust to hear their story."

Sometime later we found ourselves sitting a distance from the hotel. Slowly but surely, we began telling Charlie our story, which I was sure he would find impossible to believe. I started by telling him about the incident when I got mad at my mother and told her I hated her only to find the following morning she had disappeared.

"I learned the hard way that words are powerful," I said. "They are like weapons. Once they are released, they can't be taken back."

"Charlie, this will be hard for you to believe," Presley said next. "We're from the 21st century. We've traveled through time. Where we are from, automobiles carrying people and speeding up to one hundred miles an hour are commonplace. There are machines called computers that give access to endless information. Some of it is good, but some of it is bad. Almost everyone has one. In our world, we have objects called cell phones that allow us to communicate with people everywhere, even in other countries, any time. They are commonplace, too."

"With all of that, why would you want to come here?" Charlie asked.

"We don't know why we landed here," I said. "We were searching for my mother, but once we got here, we felt completely at home."

"Things are not all good in the 21st century," Presley said. "We are dealing with problems that are hard for us to comprehend. There's terrible pollution, climate change, traffic jams, and crowding. A lot of kids are being raised by single parents, and many of them spend all their time staring at their computers or cell phones. They hardly ever go outside. A lot of the food in our world is full of chemicals. The food we have eaten in your world is delicious. People may live longer in our world, but there is a lot of sickness. Having spent time in your world, in some ways, I like it better. People aren't as busy, and in many ways, your life is simpler."

"There are terrible wars in our world, too," Amy said. "My village in Sudan was attacked, and to save our lives, we had to run to refugee camps. A lot of us died."

"I thought the Civil War was the worst war mankind has ever

seen," Charlie said, looking confused. "Why were you attacked?" he asked Amy.

"The government claimed it was about religion, but they really wanted our resources. Even though your country has dealt with wars, it is still the safest and best place to live. My mother and I are grateful the United States gave us refuge."

I then told Charlie how, after my mother's disappearance, my father, who was in the military, was reported missing.

"I had to live with my mean aunt. That's how I met Amy. Dad was rescued, but we had lost all our money, so he started a travel magazine. That's how we ended up in Salado."

"We were trying to catch a tiny animal in the tree in the courtyard at the Stagecoach Inn," Presley continued. "We fell and landed in prehistoric Texas. Sophie's mom saved us when we almost got killed. She insisted we go back to our present time."

"When we got back to the 21st century, no one believed us," I continued, "not even my father. Determined to find my mother again, we climbed the tree. When we fell, we ended up in your time."

"That's why you were dressed the way you were. Don't tell me that is how people dress in your world," Charlie added, a look of alarm on his face.

We all laughed. "Sometimes," I added, "but we have nice clothes, too. Most of the adults dress more conservatively. Women have the right to vote, and many have high-paying jobs, like my mother. They even wear pants, as well as dresses. They don't wear corsets, and they don't use potions on their skin that contain arsenic, so they don't get poisoned."

"My mother wears high heels. They're almost as bad," Presley said with a disgusted look on his face.

He looked a little embarrassed when Amy and I both laughed. "Don't knock those high heels," I said. "Mom had several pair. I think they're beautiful, and I plan to wear them as soon as I'm old enough."

"Not me. I'm too tall as it is," Amy said.

After we were finished talking, Charlie was silent for several minutes. "I don't know why, but I believe you," he said. "Earlier on, I would have thought this was all hogwash, and you were liars or just plumb loco, but a lot of things are starting to make sense."

Turning to my mother, he said, "I thought you were an angel when I first saw you, and I still do. You're just not like the angels I've seen in picture books. When Bess and I pulled these kids out of the tunnel, it was blocked by a cave-in that totally sealed the entrance. You walked out without a scratch carrying Sophie's pets. That was not humanly possible."

With that, he turned and headed toward the stable. "Don't worry," he yelled over his shoulder. "I won't tell anyone. They wouldn't believe it anyway." As he walked away, he was rubbing his eyes. "Maybe I'm dreaming," I heard him mutter.

Catching Amy's eye, Presley said, "Let's you and I go for a walk. I think Sophie and her mother need to talk." With that, he and Amy walked away arm in arm.

With Bingo sitting quietly at my feet and Bo Jangles nestled in my mother's arms, we proceeded to do just that.

Chapter 13

"I am so ashamed," I said after Amy and Presley left. "I wanted to find that gold even though I knew it was stolen. I almost got all of us killed. Because we arrived after the Civil War, many of the people in Salado are so poor they barely have enough to eat. I thought once we found the gold, we could help them."

"Your intentions were good," Mom said. "I think you've learned a lesson. Stolen goods need to be returned to their rightful owners. There's another kind of gold in Texas. It's black, and it's underground. People here may not know it yet, but it will make Texas incredibly rich."

"Can I tell people about it when we get back to the hotel?" I asked hopefully.

"No, dear. You'll be leaving. You're not coming back to this time period."

Hearing those words, I thought my heart would break. I started to cry again. "I can't give up Isadora. She's so adorable. I love her, and I know she loves me. She's like the little sister I never had. Presley is Tom's hero. What will they do without us?"

"Isadora and Tom will be fine. They will miss you at first. As I said, time moves forward. Have you noticed how often the new sheriff has been coming into the hotel? He hopes to see Miss Elizabeth. They will get married and have a baby girl. Isadora will be a big sister to that child in the same way you've been a big sister to her. Tom will grow up to have integrity and courage, never forgetting Presley's example."

"I still wish I could have helped people," I said wistfully.

"You don't realize how much you've done. You've even made an impact on a woman who didn't like children or animals. She was very set in her ways."

Puzzled at first, I suddenly remembered Miss Teakins. Thinking back to our short encounter, I believed her only goal was to get as far away from me as possible, especially when I found out she chewed snuff.

As if reading my mind, Mother laughed. "She's not only gotten a cat she dotes on, she has adopted an orphan. Without you, Presley, and your pets, I doubt she would have ever changed, and that would have been sad. People who refuse to change often find themselves stuck in time."

Hearing her words, my mind turned to the men who wanted to kill us. I shuddered. "Are some people born evil?" I asked. "Like Killer Miller and Apache Kid?"

"I don't think so. Those two had a lot of heartbreak growing up just like so many others. Instead of growing through their experiences, they became consumed by hatred, and their actions were so horrendous they brought about their own destruction."

Mother smiled again, "The three of you have no idea how many lives you've touched. Kate had hardened her heart, leaving room only for Doc Holliday. Because of yours and Presley's actions, she opened her heart to Amy. Charlie finally was able to learn to trust and unburden himself by revealing his secret. His life has been very difficult. He has to be on guard constantly."

"Will people find out he's a woman?"

"Not until he dies, and it will be a shock. When it comes to light that he voted in the national election, the authorities will be outraged. Even so, he will go down in history as the most famous stagecoach driver in the West."

"Can you see into the future? Do you know what will happen to us?"

"I can see fragments of both the past and the future because time is circular," Mother replied. "Amy will start a non-profit foundation and build a hospital in Sudan. Presley, of course, will be a concert pianist. He also will write songs that will become popular all over the world."

"I'm just average. I'm not gifted like Presley. I know you remember that I just got average grades in school. I probably won't do anything unusual."

"Just as you thought, you will become a writer. Because you have so much empathy, you will put your heart and soul into what you write. People will tell you secrets they would never think of telling anyone. What you write will have tremendous influence."

"Everyone has gifts," Mom added, "but sadly, many people never explore them. They lead average lives because they are so afraid of failure they refuse to take chances."

I began to realize that maybe I was not average after all. At an earlier time, I would have dismissed what my mother said simply because she was my mother. Like all mothers, when it comes to their children, they tend to be unrealistic. But I now knew, without a shadow of a doubt, my mother was not unrealistic and that she would never lie to me.

"What about Dad? Will he ever be happy again?"

For just a minute I saw a shadow of sadness cross my mother's face. "Yes," she finally replied, "but he is about to face his biggest test. He's a born warrior, and he will find it very hard to get through these coming months. Only you can comfort him."

Alarmed I asked, "What will happen to him."

"I can't tell you now, but you will know soon."

"You loved each other so much. This is one of the reasons I wanted you to come back with me."

"I can't. Your father will come to realize I am always with him, just as I'm always with you."

More confused than ever, I wanted to ask her to explain, but she said, "It's time for us to go back to the hotel."

Thinking about climbing that tree again, I felt apprehensive as I remembered how Presley and I found ourselves dealing with hostile crows on our last trip in time.

Again, my mother seemed to read my mind. "Don't worry about the tree," she laughed. "Your tree climbing days are over."

I started to ask her what she meant, but I stopped when I saw Amy and Presley headed our way. With Bingo walking with Presley and Bo Jangles in my arms, we started walking back to the Stagecoach Inn. When I turned to ask my mother another question, she was gone.

Chapter 14

"I've lost her again," I thought as tears came to my eyes. It was then I heard a whisper. "Remember, I'm with you always."

As I continued to walk, I began to understand. "I think what my mother was trying to tell me is that even when our bodies die, our spirits live on," I told Presley.

I was still deep in thought when Presley yelled, "Wow! I don't know if I'm freaking ready for this."

Startled I looked up and jumped back as a car sped by. "How did we get this far from the Stagecoach Inn?" I wondered aloud.

"It seems like we've been walking forever," Amy said.

"You might say that," Presley said. "Without knowing how, we've moved from the 1800s back to the 21st century, and this time we didn't even have to climb the tree."

As we neared the Stagecoach Inn, I was startled to see several police cars and a light-colored van in the driveway. Peering out the van windows were adorable black children ranging in ages from a toddler to ten. "Those are my sisters," Amy said. "My mother must be here."

"Presley, do you think we're in trouble? We've been gone for weeks," I asked.

"Maybe so," Presley replied as he looked at the police cars.

Just then, Presley's mother and his grandfather came rushing toward us.

"We've been looking for you. You need to come back to the hotel.

We're meeting in my father's office," Charlotte said. To my surprise, when she looked at me, she had tears in her eyes.

"What is going on?" I wondered before being momentarily distracted when Amy's mother, dressed in a colorful dress and turban, joined us.

Turning to Amy, Charlotte said, "Your mother was worried. I told her I thought she was mistaken when she insisted you were here. I realize I was the one who was mistaken. Did you arrive today?"

"Yes, ma'am. I got in early. I didn't want to wake you."

"Let's go home, Amy," her mother said. "Your friends have a lot to deal with right now." Before leaving, she took my hand. "I'm so glad you're Amy's friend."

"Believe me, next to Presley, Amy's the best friend I've ever had," I said fervently.

"I like her, too," Presley said.

"I'll be praying for you, dear," Amy's mother said before they walked away.

Confused, I was becoming apprehensive. Something was wrong. I needed to find my father.

As Presley's mother turned back to me, it was obvious she was too distracted to stop to wonder how Amy managed to arrive without anyone knowing. It was also obvious that while we believed we had been gone for weeks during our visit to the 1800s, in this world, we had only been gone for a couple of hours.

Putting her arm around me, Charlotte steered me toward the hotel. At the same time, Presley's grandfather Patrick took him aside. I could hear him talking to Presley in a low voice.

Suddenly, I felt almost paralyzed with fear. I didn't want to walk into the hotel and sit in Patrick's office because I knew I would hear something terrible. Yet, mutely, I allowed Presley's mother to steer me across the lobby. When I entered Patrick's office, the fact that Dad's friend and editor Mike was there, along with two police officers and a man that would later prove to be a private detective, barely registered because all of my attention was on my father. Slumped in a chair, he had his head in his hands as tears splashed onto his lap.

Looking up at me, he said, "They found your mother. She's been murdered."

I screamed. "No, she's hasn't! I've seen her. She's fine."

Looking wordlessly at me, my father's eyes showed utter sorrow.

Without another word, I ran out of the hotel, weeping. Moments later, I found myself standing under the tree in the courtyard. Ageless, its trunk was as huge as I remembered, and as the leaves danced in the wind, it looked so inviting I decided to climb it again. For a moment, I almost believed the tree was calling me. I didn't know where I would land this time, but it didn't matter because I wanted to be any place but here. Not only did I feel broken apart by grief, I felt rage more intense than anything I could have ever imagined.

I turned to find Presley standing next to me. Looking at me with compassion, he said, "It won't bring her back, Sophie. I think Charlie was right. She's an angel. But if you're determined to climb that tree, I'm coming with you."

Indecisive, I looked down to see Bingo and Bo Jangles sitting at my feet. As Bingo let out a long, drawn-out howl, Bo Jangles uttered a pitiful meow. Somehow, in their amazing canine and feline minds, my loyal pets knew my heart was breaking. Of course, I would take them with me because we couldn't bear to be separated. Then my mind went back to that nightmarish event when I thought they had both been killed in the tunnel cave-in on our final day in the 1800s. I had almost gotten them killed. I wouldn't do that to them again.

"Be strong. Your father needs you. Remember, even if you can't see me, I am with you." Even though I couldn't see her, my mother's voice was so clear that she could have been standing next to me.

"Did I just imagine that?" I wondered. "No," I decided. She had spoken clearly.

"Thank you, Presley. You are such a loyal friend. I need to go to my father."

"Are you sure you're OK?" he asked, with a look of concern on his face.

"Yes, I'm fine now. We both saw her. She's an angel, and that is something that will always bring me comfort."

With that, I turned, walked into the hotel, crossed the lobby, and went into Patrick's office. Sitting down next to my father, I took his hand. "I'm sorry," I said. "I shouldn't have done that." Turning to the detective, I asked, "What happened."

Chapter 15

It was a horrific tale. Apparently, when Bill Crankshaw had started draining funds from my mother's publishing company, she had hired a private detective even though my father had asked her to wait until he got home. Within a short time, the detective gave her a detailed report that showed Bill Crankshaw's name was an alias. There was a strong suspicion that by using different names, faking resumes and impressive backgrounds, he moved across the country focusing on wealthy women who were alone. Once he had all their money, he would move on.

"Why my mother?" I asked.

"It was common knowledge that your mother's publishing company was successful," the detective replied. "It wasn't hard for Crankshaw to find out your father was in the military, which caused him to be absent for months at a time. He also found out she was seeking a partner to help run the business because she wanted to devote more time to you."

My heart sank. Was I the cause of my mother's death?

As if reading my mind, the detective said, "Don't blame yourself. Psychopaths like Crankshaw can be very convincing. They exude superficial charm. Your mother had a good heart. Because she was such a good person, she found it hard to believe there are people who are downright evil. We think that when Crankshaw realized your mother was about to expose him, he waited one night until he knew she was asleep. He also knew Bingo would be in your room."

"I think this could be my fault," I said. I then told the detective about that fateful night when, despite Bingo trying to warn me, I thought the noise I heard was from a branch brushing against the window.

Lifting his head, my father looked at me and said, "Sophie, none of this is your fault. If it's anyone's fault, it's mine. I should have been there."

"But you couldn't. You were in Afghanistan."

"Besides that," one of the cops said, "if you had gone in to check on your mother, Crankshaw probably would have killed you, too."

"We now believe he came in through a window," the detective continued. "After he kidnapped your mother, he told her he would kill you if she didn't cooperate."

"So that's why she turned over the deed to the house and signed documents giving him everything," Dad said.

"Yes. Then, after killing her, he wrapped her in a blanket and drove to the co-op garden on Fitzhugh. He knew that area is deserted at that time of night, and in his sick mind, it was revenge because your mother had gone against his wishes and featured the garden in a cover story in her magazine. He buried her at the back of the garden."

"We never would have known if it were not for those Vietnamese gardeners finding her earring," the other officer said.

"He couldn't kill my mother's spirit," I thought. "She was not only good she was strong enough to leave a clue."

"When the gardeners brought me Rachel's earring, I knew immediately it was hers," Mike said. "It even had her initials engraved on the back."

"They were her favorite. She wore them every day," I said.

"At first I couldn't get anyone to take me seriously," Mike continued, "but the gardeners kept returning. They were scared. They talked about strange events occurring at the co-op. They claimed the vegetables and fruit at the back of the garden grew huge, almost overnight. They even claimed they had seen a lady in white watching their children as they played. I didn't believe in ghosts, and at first, I thought they were just superstitious. After a time, I had to accept the fact there was something going on. It was as if Rachael was waiting for me to act. I finally convinced the police to dig up the back of the garden. That's when they found her."

Sitting quietly, struggling not to cry again, I tried to push away the image in my mind of my mother's body being exhumed. Then, looking at Mike, the police, and the detective, I said, "He may have killed her body, but he couldn't destroy her spirit. She's too strong."

"Where is that bastard?" my father asked. "I want to strangle him with my bare hands."

"Leave that to us," one of the cops warned. "He's presumed innocent until proven guilty, according to the law. He's fallen off the grid, but we'll find him."

"I'm used to seeking out an enemy that I can see," Dad said. "I don't know how I can deal with this."

I stood up and, standing in front of my father, I cupped his face in my hands. "I was told that when people are completely evil, they self-destruct," I said. "You have to believe me. She's still with us."

"I wish it were true, Sophie," he said with tears in his eyes.

"It is. You'll see. A love like Mom's never dies."

Chapter 16

The next few days were like a whirlwind. Charlotte took charge in arranging the memorial service. The day after the police and detective came to the Stagecoach Inn, the newspaper in Dallas ran a front-page story about Mom's murder. The story was picked up nationwide and was on all the radio stations and television channels. Mom's friends were interviewed, and during a CNN television interview by Anderson Cooper, Mom's best friend Stephanie looked directly into the camera and said, "We all knew Chris was innocent. He adored Rachael. It's disgusting what he and his child have been put through. It's about time the police acted. Hopefully, they'll find that horrible man and bring him to justice."

The entire city of Dallas rallied around us, and little by little, I could feel my father getting stronger. One day, as he was sitting next to me in the lobby of the hotel we were staying in, I saw a faraway look in his eyes. When he clenched his jaw, I knew instinctively that mentally he was hunting Bill Crankshaw. After watching those emotions play across his face, I saw him smile. It was a grim smile, and I realized, in his imagination, he had just caught him.

"I have to help him through this," I thought. Getting up, I hugged him. "Remember, she's still with us. She loves us as much or even more than ever."

"I hope so," was his sad response. As hours went by, I began to see a flicker of hope in his eyes as he thought about what I said.

In the interim, Charlotte, her father Patrick, and Presley came to Dallas, and we went out to dinner.

"Chris, you've made quite an impression during your stay at our hotel," Patrick said. "The whole town is aware of what happened to your wife. The mayor called and wanted me to tell you they are all there for you."

"Yes," Presley's mom said. "Dad and I have been talking. Sophie has been so good for Presley. She's really brought him out of his shell. We'd like you to consider living at the hotel. You can use one of the conference rooms for your business. I know it's no fun living in a hotel room, so we'll set up a suite."

"You'll never be hungry," Presley said hopefully. "Will you do it?"

"Since your magazine is gaining in popularity, you will have to travel more," Patrick said. "I know it will ease your mind knowing Sophie is staying with us. School will start shortly. I think you should enroll her."

"Thank you," Dad said. "That's tempting. Sophie and I can't bear driving past our old house in East Dallas. People here mean well, but we are constantly getting calls. So many strangers stop us on the streets it's almost impossible to go anywhere."

Just like that, it was settled. My dad and I, along with our pets, would become permanent residents of Salado.

A lot of people assumed Mom's memorial service would be held at a large church in an affluent neighborhood, but Dad and I both insisted it he held at the church Mom loved. It was a small, old adobe-style church on Greenville Avenue.

On the day of the service, we knew we'd made the right decision. A large, framed picture of Mom had been placed on an easel near the podium. The entire front of the church was almost buried in flowers. As Bingo and Bo Jangles sat quietly at my feet, I could hear more and more people arriving. As I turned, I saw Mr. and Mrs. Jones walking up the aisle. Then, feeling a tap on my shoulder, I turned, and there was Uncle Bob. He shook Dad's hand and gave me a hug. Next to him was Aunt Rose and Mabel. Mabel leaned over and whispered, "I see a light around you Sophie. I told you you were a Star Child."

Aunt Rose was not able to look directly at me. I think she was ashamed of the way she had treated me. No longer angry, I felt sorry for her. Because they were what little family we had left, they sat at the end of the pew. Of course, Charlotte, Patrick, and Presley were there with us. When Amy and her mother, both clad in their African dresses and turbans, walked up the aisle, I could hear people gasp. Amy was standing tall. For once, she did not seem to be embarrassed about her height. "I wonder if someone's approached her about modeling?" I thought to myself.

Before long, there was no standing room left. The audience had spilled out into the small front yard. Anticipating this, the church personnel had put up outside speakers.

At first, the service was what you might describe as standard as the minister recited the basics about mother, talking about her contributions to the city and how much she was loved. Then Mike, who was sitting behind us, stood up.

"I'd like to say something," he announced. When the minister nodded, he said, "Rachael was the best boss I've ever had. She was not hardboiled like so many publishers today. She never lost her kind heart. Not only was she creative and talented, she was funny. She also had the worst sense of direction of anyone I've ever known."

People laughed.

After Mike's comments, it was like a dam broke. One by one, others got up and spoke, including one of the Vietnamese gardeners who described how mother visited weekly when she was alive and even wrote a story about them. "Very good for business," he added, before sitting down.

To my surprise, Dad walked up to the podium. In a clear voice, he told the audience how he met Mom. Then his voice quavered a little as he talked about her beauty, not only on the outside but on the inside as well. He revealed it was his love for her that kept him from giving up when his helicopter crashed in Afghanistan because he was determined to get home to her and to me. "I believe Sophie is correct," was the last thing he said. "Rachel is an angel. Sophie's convinced she's not really gone, and when I think about it, I think she's right." When he returned to our pew. there was not a dry eye in the chapel.

To my surprise, Presley stood up and went to the black, baby grand piano. Sitting down, he looked directly at me. "Sophie, this is for you and your mother. I've composed this for both of you." With that, he closed his eyes, and with a look of rapture on his face, he began to play. The music, at times, soared. At other times, it was almost a whisper. As I listened, I was taken back in time. I could see the still waters of ponds, waterfalls, creeks, grazing deer, and soaring birds. I could see strange creatures, wonderful and terrifying, that were no longer part of the modern world.

Looking down, I saw Bingo and Bo Jangles, with their noses and ears tilted forward, staring intently at the area by the piano. When I saw what they were looking at, I froze. Mother was standing directly behind Presley, but she wasn't alone. In a group on the other side of the piano stood Doc Holliday. Next to him was Kate, Aunt Elizabeth, Tom, and Isadora. Charlie, wearing his typical disguise, gave me a wide smile. Standing next to him was the Widow Teakins. A little girl was shyly peeking around her skirts. Holding a large, ginger-colored, self-satisfied looking cat in her arms, the widow looked directly at me and, moving her jaw slightly, winked. She was chewing snuff!

Blinking, I looked again. They were gone, but in my heart, I knew they were not really gone. I realized I had just experienced a minute in time that was magical, a magic that was, in fact, reality. The reality is that we are all connected by love, a love that defies death.

As the music reached a crescendo, my heart lifted. I thought back to the time when I got so angry, I decided I didn't believe in God. Mabel was right. Even when I didn't believe in God, God believed in me.

I glanced over at Dad and saw that he was sitting erect. At that moment, the look on his face was one of pride. He had loved and had been loved by a woman worth loving, a woman not only who he loved, but who many others loved as well.

I took his hand. "Isn't it wonderful how many people loved Mom?" I whispered. "She was so wonderful. I just hope I can grow up to be like her."

Looking at me, he smiled. "You will. You are already on your way."

"It will be a big adjustment, but we'll get through this," I whispered.

"God willing," he said.

"Yes," I answered. "I think He is."

The End

Afterword

I've always believed that truth can often be stranger than fiction. In the case of Sophie's Adventure in Time this is certainly true. Even though this story is fiction it contains many authentic facts and true life colorful characters (some good, others bad) who make the history of the Wild West so interesting.

Lakewood in Dallas, where the story starts out, is one of the oldest neighborhoods in Dallas. With many old stately homes it has maintained a strong sense of neighborhood charm.

The Stage Coach Inn, located in the picturesque town of Salado, is a popular stopping place for visitors. There are various trees on the grounds of the hotel that have been reputed to be at least six hundred years old.

In **Part 1** when Sophie and Presley find themselves in prehistoric Texas, the world they knew is not only different, it's beautiful and extremely dangerous. Much of Texas at that time was covered by a shallow sea. The tiny animal (Gizmo) that Sophie and Presley were chasing was a Crusafontia. They populated the southwest. The flying dinosaur that nearly killed Sophie and Presley was a Ptorosaurs. The Saber Toothed Tiger existed millions of years before this time period, but being a cat lover I could not resist bringing this beautiful animal forward and incorporating it into this story.

In **Part ll** I've tried to give the reader a glimpse of the difficulties of life in the south after the Civil War. One fascinating character was Doc Holliday who was a dentist, which earned him the nickname Doc. A gambler and gun fighter he was known for his hot temper. He did, at one time, have an office in Dallas, Texas, but because he had consumption (tuberculosis) he coughed continually, which alarmed his patients. He wandered around the west until he eventually hooked up with his friend Wyatt Earp.

Big Nose Kate's real name was Mary Katherine Haroney. Born in Budapest her father was a wealthy physician who eventually moved the family to South America. When she arrived in Dodge City she called herself Kate Elder. She spoke several languages. She loved Doc Holliday and when he was confined to his room in a hotel she set fire to a shed and helped him escape. They both eventually joined Wyatt Earp in Dodge City. Kate Elder had a very colorful life.

The little Sudanese girl Amy in now an adult living in Dallas, Texas. I met her as a child when I was writing the book Dark Exodus, the Lost Girls of Sudan.

Sugar Foot's real name was Tom Brewster. In his teens he took a correspondence course to become a lawyer. When he came west to be a cowboy his lack of skill and ineptness earned him the nickname of Sugar Foot, which was one step lower than a Tender Foot. He turned to crime and was killed by Charlie Parkhurst when he tried to rob the stage.

Charlie Parkhurst was a female and managed to disguise herself until her death. Born Charlene Parkhurst she was in an orphanage in New Hamphire, which she hated. Disguising herself as a boy she ran away when she was 15. She became a famous stage coach driver known for her skill with horses and her cool head under pressure. She shot Black Bart (another outlaw) and filled his backside with buckshot when he tried to rob her. She also blinded and killed Sugar Foot. While disguised as a man she is the first woman to vote in a national election. Since my maiden name is Parkhurst I hope we may be related. Although her life took place in California I couldn't resist moving her to Texas and incorporating her into this story.

The Jesse James Brothers were famous outlaws who are featured in stories and movies to this day.

Outlaw Sam Bass robbed the Union Pacific and got away with sixty thousand dollars in gold coins and silver bullion, which has never been found. Rumor has it that it is buried somewhere on the grounds of the

Stagecoach Inn. When he murdered Deputy Grimes in cold blood in Round Rock, Texas. Major Jones, who was getting a shave at the time heard the shots. He ran outside (still with lather on his face) and shot Bass who died from the wounds.

Probably the worst outlaw was Jim Miller. He murdered his grandparents when he was eight years old. Because he saw himself as a preacher he didn't drink, smoke or swear, which earned him one of two nick names. One was Preacher Jim. The other was Killer Jim. He was a hired killer and a true psychopath who killed more than 22 people. When he assassinated a former deputy US Marshall he was hung in Ada, Oklahoma by an enraged mob.